Curious, I strode toward it.

When I got to the gate, I realized it was a cemetery, a family burial plot. Some of its gravestones looked extremely old, round-shouldered and leaning forward as if they were tired, their names and dates no longer readable. There were new markers made of shiny rock, and I strolled over to look at them. *Thomas Barnes,* I read. My mother's father. I touched his stone lightly. *Avril Scarborough.* I didn't know that name. I looked at the dates, drew back, then did the math again. Sixteen, as old as me. Did she have any idea she'd die that young?

The grave gave me an eerie feeling. I didn't want to touch her stone, and turned, suddenly compelled to get out of there. As I did, I gave a quick glance back at the house. The lowering sun flared off the paned glass, but I saw it, the movement of someone stepping back from the window, as if trying not to be seen. After a moment I realized the person had been watching from my bedroom. I walked toward the house, but the reflected light made it impossible to see in.

A vague uneasiness seeped into me. Aside from the invitation itself, Grandmother and Matt acted as if they had no interest in getting to know me. But obviously, someone was interested enough to keep a secret eye on me. . . .

DARK SECRETS
Legacy of Lies

Elizabeth Chandler

AN ARCHWAY PAPERBACK
Published by POCKET BOOKS
New York London Toronto Sydney Singapore

This book is a work of fiction. Names, characters, places and incidents are products of the author's imagination or are used fictitiously. Any resemblance to actual events or locales or persons, living or dead, is entirely coincidental.

AN ARCHWAY PAPERBACK *Original*

 An Archway Paperback published by
POCKET BOOKS, a division of Simon & Schuster, Inc.
1230 Avenue of the Americas, New York, NY 10020

Copyright © 2000 by Mary Claire Helldorfer

ISBN: 0-7434-0028-3

First Archway Paperback printing October 2000

10 9 8 7 6 5 4 3

DARK SECRETS is a trademark of Simon & Schuster, Inc.

AN ARCHWAY PAPERBACK and colophon are registered trademarks of Simon & Schuster, Inc.

Front cover illustration by Sandy Young/Studio Y
Book design by Jaime Putorti

Printed in the U.S.A.

IL 6+

one

Last night I visited the house again. It looked as it did ten years ago, when I dreamed about it often. I've never seen the house in real life, at least not that I can remember. It is tall, three stories of paned windows, all brick with a shingle roof. The part I remember most clearly is the covered porch. No wider than the front steps, it has facing benches that I like to sit on. I guess I was never shy, not even at six; in the dream I always opened the door, walked inside, and played with the toys.

Last night the door was locked. That's how I awoke, trying with all my strength to open it, desperate to get inside. Something was wrong, but now I can't say what. Was there something dangerous outside the house from which I was fleeing? Was there a person in the house who needed my help? It was as if the first part of my dream was missing. But one thing I knew for sure: Someone on the other side of the door was trying hard to keep me out.

"I'm not going," I had told my father back in June. "She's a mean old lady. She disowned Mom and won't speak to you. She has never had anything to do with Pete, Dave, or me. Why should I have anything to do with her?"

"For your mother's sake," he'd said.

Several months later I was on a flight from Arizona to Maryland, still resisting my grandmother's royal command to visit. I took out her invitation, the first message I'd received from her in my life, and reread it— two sentences, sounding as stiff as a textbook exercise.

Dear Megan,
  This summer I will see you at Scarborough House.
I have enclosed a check to cover airfare.

                          Regards,
              Helen Scarborough Barnes

Well, I hadn't expected "love and kisses" from a woman who cut off her only daughter when she had decided to marry someone a different color. My mother, coming from a deep-rooted Eastern Shore family, has more English blood in her than Prince Charles. My father, also from an old Maryland family, is African-American. After trying to have children of their own, they adopted me, then my two brothers. It would be naive to expect warmth from a person who refused to consider adopted kids her grandchildren.

Now that I thought about it, the meaning of my dream the night before was pretty obvious, even the feeling that something was wrong. The door to my mother's family had always been closed to me; when a door kept locked for sixteen years suddenly, without explanation, opens, you can't help but wonder what you're walking into.

"Megan? You made it!" the woman said, crumpling up the sign with my name on it, then giving me a big hug. "I'm Ginny Lloyd, your mother's best old friend." She laughed. "I guess you figured that out."

When Ginny heard I was coming, she'd insisted on meeting me at the airport close to Baltimore. That October day we loaded my luggage into the back of her ancient green station wagon, pushing aside bags of old sweaters, skirts, shoes, and purses—items she had picked up to sell in her vintage clothes shop.

"I hope you don't mind the smell of mothballs," Ginny said.

"No problem," I replied.

"How about the smell of a car burning oil?"

"That's okay, too."

"We can open the windows," she told me. "Of course, the muffler's near gone."

I laughed. Blond and freckled, she had the same southernish accent as my mother. I felt comfortable with her right away.

When I was buckled in, Ginny handed me a map so I could follow our progress toward Wisteria, which is on the Eastern Shore of the Chesapeake Bay.

"It's about a two-hour drive," she said. "I told Mrs. Barnes I'd have you at Scarborough House well before dark."

"I'm getting curious," I told her. "When Mom left Maryland, she didn't bring any pictures with her. I've seen a few photos that my uncle Paul sent, showing him and Mom playing when they were little, but you can't see the house in them. What's it like?"

"What has your mother told you about it?" Ginny asked.

"Not much. There's a main house with a back wing. It's old."

"That's about it," Ginny said.

It was a short answer from a person who had spent a lot of time there as a child and teenager—nearly as short as my mother's answers about the place.

"Oh, and it's haunted," I added.

"People say that," Ginny replied.

I looked at her, surprised. I had been joking.

"Of course, every old house on the Shore has its ghost stories," she added quickly. "Just keep the lights on if it feels spooky."

This trip might turn out to be more interesting than I thought.

Ginny turned on the radio, punching in a country station. I opened the map she had given me and studied it. The Sycamore River cut into the Eastern Shore at an angle. If you were traveling up the Chesapeake Bay, you'd enter the wide river mouth of the Sycamore and head in a northeasterly direction. On the right, close to the mouth, you'd see a large creek named Wist. The next creek up is Oyster. The town of Wisteria sits between them, nearly surrounded by water, the Sycamore River on one side and the creeks on the other two. As for my grandmother's property, it was the large point of land below the town, washed on one side by Wist Creek and on the other side by the Sycamore.

We crossed two sets of railroad tracks. I watched the scenery change from outlet stores to fields of corn and soy and low horizons of trees. The sky was half the world on the Eastern Shore. Ginny asked a lot of questions and seemed more interested in talking about life in Tucson than life in Wisteria.

"What's my grandmother like?" I asked at last.

For a full minute the only response was the roar of the car engine.

"She's, uh, different," Ginny said. "We're coming up on Oyster Creek. Wisteria's just on the other side."

"Different how?" I persisted.

"She has her own way of seeing things. She can be fierce at times."

"Do people like her?"

Ginny hesitated. "Have you spent much time in a small town?" she asked.

"No."

"Small-town folks are like a big family living in one

house. They can be real friendly and helpful, but they can also say nasty things about each other and squabble a lot."

She hadn't answered my question about how others saw my grandmother, but I could figure it out. She wasn't the town favorite.

We rumbled over the metal grating of the drawbridge. I hung my head out the window for a moment. In Tucson, creeks were often just trickles. This one was the width of a river.

"We're on Scarborough Street now," Ginny said. "The streets off to our right lead down to the commercial docks, where the oyster and crab boats are. The streets to the left border the college. In a few blocks we'll be crossing over High Street, which is Main Street for us. Want to drive down it?"

"Sure."

We passed a school, went a block farther, then took a right onto High. The street had a mix of houses, churches, and small shops, all of the buildings made of brick or wood. Some of the houses edged right up to the sidewalk; a few had tiny plots of grass in front of them. Pots of bright chrysanthemums perched on windowsills and steps. The sidewalks on both sides of High Street were brick and ripply, especially around the roots of the sycamore trees that lined the street. But even where there weren't roots, the brick looked softened, as if the footprints of two and a half centuries had been worn into it.

"It's pretty," I said. "Are there a lot of wisteria vines around here?"

"People grow it," she said, "but actually, the parcel of land that became the town was won in a card game called whist. That was the town's original name. Some upright folks in the 1800s, who didn't approve of gambling, added to it. I guess we're lucky they weren't playing Crazy Eights."

I laughed.

"There's my shop, Yesterdaze." Ginny slowed down and pointed to a storefront with a large, paned window that bowed out over the sidewalk. "Next door is Tea Leaves. Jamie, the owner, makes pastries to die for.

"The town harbor is ahead of us," she went on. "Only pleasure boats dock there now. I'm going to swing around to Bayview Avenue and show you where I live. You know you're welcome to stay with me if things get difficult."

"Difficult how?" I asked.

She shrugged. "I find it isolated out there on the other side of the Wist. And Scarborough House seems awfully big without a family to fill it up."

"Is that why my grandmother invited me? She can't get anybody else to come?"

"I doubt *that's* the reason. Mrs. Barnes has never liked company– Whoa!" Ginny exclaimed, hitting her brakes hard, sending shoe boxes tumbling over the seat from the back of the station wagon.

A guy in an open-topped Jeep, impatient to get

around a car making a turn, had suddenly cut in front of us. The backseat passengers of the red Jeep, two girls and a guy, held on to one another and hooted. The girl in the front seat turned briefly to look at us, laughing and tossing her long hair. The driver didn't acknowledge his near miss.

"Jerk," I said aloud.

Ginny looked amused. "That was your cousin."

"My cousin?" I twisted in my seat, to look down the side street where the Jeep had made another sudden turn.

"Matt Barnes," she replied.

"I thought he was in Chicago."

"Your uncle moved there, and Matt's mother is somewhere in the North, I believe."

"Boston," I told her. It had been an ugly divorce, I knew that much.

"Matt has spent nearly every summer in Wisteria. He transferred to the high school here last winter and is living full-time with your grandmother. You didn't know that?"

I shook my head.

"She bought him the Jeep this past summer. Rumor has it he's getting his own boat. Matt's usually carting around jocks or girls."

Spoiled and wild, I thought. But things were looking up. No matter what he was like, spending two weeks with a guy my own age was better than being alone with a fierce seventy-six-year-old. I'd just fasten my seat belt and go along for the ride.

"Does my grandmother drive?" I asked.

"Pretty much like Matt," Ginny replied, laughing.

When we got to Bayview, she pointed out her house, a soft yellow cottage with gray shutters, then returned to Scarborough Road.

We crossed the Wist, rumbling over an old bridge, drove about a quarter mile more, then turned right between two brick pillars. The private road that led to my grandmother's started out paved, but crumbled into gravel and dirt. Tall, conical cedar trees lined both sides. They did not bend gracefully over the drive, as trees do in pictures of southern mansions, but stood upright, like giant green game pieces. At the end of the double row of trees I saw sections of sloping gray roof and brick chimneys, four of them.

"We're coming up behind the house," Ginny said. "The driveway loops around to the front. You're seeing the back wing. That picket fence runs along the herb garden by the kitchen."

"The house is huge."

"Remember that you are welcome to stay with me," she said.

"Thanks, but I'll be fine."

Now that I was here, I was looking forward to the next two weeks. I mean, how much of a terror could one little old woman be? It'd be fun to explore the old house and its land, especially with a cousin my age. Four hundred acres of fields and woods and waterfront—it seemed unbelievable that I didn't have to share them with other hikers in a state park. A wave of excitement and confidence washed over me. Then Ginny circled the house and parked in front.

"Megan," she said, after a moment of silence, "Megan, are you all right?"

I nodded.

"I'll help you with your luggage."

"Thanks."

I climbed out of the car slowly, staring up at Grandmother's house. Three stories of paned windows, brick with a shingled roof, a small covered porch with facing benches—it was the house in my dreams.

I took my luggage from Ginny, feeling a little shaky. For the second time in twenty-four hours, I walked up the steps of the house. This time the door swung open.

two

"Well, what is it?" asked a short, heavyset woman whose hair was tipped orange from an old peroxide job.

"I'm here to see Mrs. Barnes." My voice sounded timid as a child's.

Ginny climbed the porch steps behind me. "Nancy, this is Megan, Mrs. Barnes's granddaughter."

Nancy's response was to turn her back and retreat into the house. I glanced questioningly at my mother's friend.

"Nancy comes in three times a week to cook and clean for your grandmother," Ginny informed me in a low voice.

"Is she always this friendly?"

" 'Fraid so."

Without stepping inside, I peered down the long,

unlit center hall. Nancy stopped at a door near the foot of the stairway, knocked, then entered. When she returned to us, she spoke to Ginny. "Mrs. Barnes wants to know how much she owes you for bringing the girl and whether you'd accept a check."

A look of surprise flickered across Ginny's face. "Please tell her it was my pleasure."

"Thanks for picking me up, Ginny," I said, slightly embarrassed.

"Sure thing. You know where to find me." She squeezed my hand and left.

Score one for Grandma, I thought as I lugged my bags inside the house: I hadn't even met her and already she'd made me feel like an inconvenience.

Nancy, having emerged a second time from the room by the stairs, fixed me with her eyes, then pointed a thumb over her shoulder. I figured it was a signal for me to go in. There was no chance to ask, since the housekeeper exited quickly through a door at the back of the hall.

I stood by the front door, considering my options. What would happen if I simply waited here? Who would give in first, me or Helen Scarborough Barnes?

I decided to take my time studying the center hall, which ran from the front door of the house to a smaller door under the main stairs, its wide plank floor covered with islands of rugs. I had never been in a hall large enough to contain sofas, side chairs, and tables. Heavy wood doors led into four rooms, two on each side. The broad staircase rose toward the back of the

house, turned and climbed several steps against the
back wall, then disappeared as it turned again toward
the front. A grandfather clock ticked on the stairway
landing: 4:25.

"Megan."

The voice was low and firm, used to being obeyed.
I took a deep breath and walked down the hall, stopping inside the frame of the door. The room was a
library, its dark walls lined with shelves of books. It
smelled of leather and old fireplace ashes. I liked it
immediately; I wish I could say the same for the
white-haired woman who sat stiff-backed behind a
desk.

She rose slowly, surprising me with her height. I
was three inches taller than my mother, and so was
she. Helen Scarborough Barnes observed me so
closely I felt as if she were counting the threads in my
clothes, adding up them and everything else she saw
to see if I passed. Fine. I could study her, too, and
decide whether she passed as a grandmother.

She had pale skin and high cheekbones. Her hair,
pulled back in a French twist, and tiny drop earrings
gave her a kind of elegance despite the fact she was
wearing slacks. I met her light blue eyes as steadily as
I could.

"You may sit down," she said.

"I'd like to stand, if you don't mind. I've been sitting all day."

There was a slight pause, then she nodded and
seated herself. "Just don't pace."

I felt an incredible urge to pace but kept it in check.

"How is your mother doing?" she asked.

"Good—*well*," I corrected my grammar. "Did you know she finished her master's degree? Last month she started a new job. She's at the same school, but as a reading specialist. She loves the kids. She's terrific with them."

I knew I was chattering.

"And your brothers?"

"They're great. Pete, who's twelve, is into music. Dave's ten and lives for sports."

"And your trip here?"

"My father's doing great, too," I said, though she hadn't asked about him. "He was honored by the Sonoran Desert Museum for his work with mammals."

"Please answer only the questions I ask," Grandmother told me.

"Just filling in the details," I responded cheerfully, though we both knew otherwise. I wasn't about to let Dad be cut out of the family.

"How was your trip here?"

"Fine."

She waited a moment, perhaps to see if I'd fill in the details. I didn't.

"I had expected you to come here in the summer, Megan."

"As Mom explained to you, I go to a year-round school and had already committed myself to working at a camp for my three-week summer break. October was the next free time."

"What is your parentage?"

The sudden question took me aback. I stared at her for a long moment. "My mother is Carolyn Barnes, my father, Kent Tilby," I said, as if that were news.

"You know what I mean, girl."

I pressed my lips together.

"Your coloring is . . . unusual," she observed.

I decided not to reply. I have straight black hair, which I keep shoulder length, gray eyes, and skin that refuses to tan. In the bronze land of Arizona, I stand out like a white mushroom, but I didn't think that was the point of her comment.

Correctly deducing that she wasn't going to get any information about my birth parents, Helen Barnes rose from her chair. "I will show you your room."

I followed her into the hall, fuming. I don't know what I had hoped for from her. An effort to get to know me, a conversation that lasted longer than three minutes and revealed some interest in me, other than genetic? Some shyness or awkwardness that told me that she, too, had intense feelings about this first meeting? There was no such sign. Her eyes could have iced over the Gulf of Mexico.

"You will see the downstairs first," she said.

I nodded. Apparently, "Would you like to?" wasn't part of her vocabulary.

She showed me the three other rooms that opened off the center hall. Like the library, each had a high ceiling and corner fireplace, but their walls were painted in bolder colors: peacock blue in the front parlor, bright mustard in the music room. The dining room, which was at the back of the main house and across the hall from the library, was blood red. All of the rooms had paintings with heavy gilt frames; the theme in the gory-colored dining room was animals and hunting. I hoped we ate in the kitchen.

"When was this house built?" I asked, abruptly turning away from an impaled deer.

"In 1720," my grandmother answered, "by a family named Winchester."

"When did our family move in?"

"The Scarboroughs bought the house, the land, and the mill in the mid-1800s."

"Is that when our family came over from England?"

"The Scarboroughs"—she said the name clearly, as if to make a distinction between that family and what I called *our* family—"have been in Maryland since the 1600s. This land was purchased by the seventh generation as a wedding gift for a son." She led the way back into the hall. "Carry whatever luggage you can," she told me, resting a thin hand on the curved banister. "Matt will bring up the rest when he gets home from his study session."

Study session? I thought. Better not mention that my cousin had come close to hitting Ginny's car when he was supposed to be hitting the books. I carried all of my luggage.

The trim in the upstairs hall was the same blue as

the parlor's, but the walls were softened by faded wallpaper. A mirror, darkened with age, hung on one wall; on another were several photographs, old tintypes. My grandmother grew impatient as I looked at them.

"Megan." She waited by the door at the top of the stairs, the only one open in the hall.

I entered and set down my bags. The square room had a fireplace in one corner and a four-poster bed in the center. Though the inside shutters had been pulled back and the windows opened, there was a musty smell, reminding me that a river was near.

"Where's the water?" I asked, quickly crossing to a window. "On the map it looked close to the house. Oh, my gosh, the trees!" I couldn't hide my enthusiasm. "I've never seen so much green, not in Tucson. Look, their tops are just turning gold."

My grandmother, not interested in looking, remained in the doorway, "You can see the creek and river when the leaves have fallen. These old homes were not built directly on the water because of the insects. Now they spray."

"Oh."

"I'll leave you to unpack," she said. "Your bathroom is through that door. Dinner is at six. If there is anything you need—"

"What am I supposed to call you?"

She hesitated.

"What does my cousin call you?" I asked.

"Grandmother."

"That's cool."

I don't think she thought so, but she didn't object. She reached back for the door handle to pull it closed behind her. "Just so we understand each other, Megan. I will respect your privacy and assume you will respect mine."

I gazed after her as she shut the door. What was *that* supposed to mean? I had been respecting her privacy for the last sixteen years. If she didn't want to open the door between us now, why had she bothered to invite me?

I glanced around the bedroom. The rooms in this house were big—formal downstairs, and simple, almost stark, upstairs. To my relief, they were nothing like the cozy room where I often played in my dream. That would have been a little too weird. There were explanations for the outward resemblance of the two houses. Mom might have described her home to me long ago, when I was too young to know I shouldn't ask about it. Or maybe I'd seen a picture of a colonial house that resembled this one. Now and then Mom subscribed to East Coast magazines that had photos of old homes. There were probably just a few basic styles.

I unpacked my clothes, then lifted out several small-framed pictures and set them on the bureau, smiling at the menagerie of people and critters. Dad's a veterinarian and Mom volunteers at an animal shelter. Our home is a small zoo, and I'm not just referring to my brothers.

I put on a clean shirt and took out a comb, running

it through my hair, then looked around the room for a mirror. Above a dressing table, where a mirror usually would hang, was a framed piece of embroidery: the Ten Commandments. Well, that's nice, I thought, a friendly reminder to guests to behave themselves! I used the mirror on the medicine cabinet in the small bath attached to my room.

As I emerged from the bathroom, I heard my cousin's Jeep circling the house. I quickly finished putting away my things and headed downstairs. At last I had someone my age to hang out with. When I reached the landing with the clock, I could hear his voice.

"She shouldn't have come. I told you before, Grandmother, it was a bad idea to invite her."

Surprised, I leaned forward to hear Grandmother's response, but she spoke too softly.

"It's just a gut feeling," my cousin said. "No, it's more than that. You haven't been acting like yourself since you first got this crazy idea."

I walked noiselessly down the steps, straining to hear Grandmother's answer, but the library door was partially closed and her voice muffled.

"I really don't care," Matt insisted loudly. "She's not my cousin—she's adopted—and you've always been the first to point that out. I can't believe you didn't tell me she was coming today. I don't know what you're up to."

This time I was close enough to hear Grandmother. "Worried?" she asked.

It was tempting to sneak up on them. But two long weeks loomed ahead and embarrassing Matt wouldn't make things easier. Give him a chance to change his mind, I told myself. I pounded down the last few steps, so they would hear me and have time to switch topics.

Grandmother was sitting at her desk again. Matt's backpack was on the floor, his back turned to me.

"Hello, Megan," Grandmother said, then glanced in Matt's direction.

"Hello," I replied, and followed her glance. Matt reached for a book high up on a shelf and began to page through it, keeping his back to me. I doubted he was as interested in the book as he pretended.

Well, okay. I could play this game. I sat down with my back to him.

"Grandmother," I said, "I was hoping you'd have some family pictures hanging up."

"There are three in the upstairs hall," she replied.

"The ones from the 1800s? They're cool. I was hoping you might have some of my grandfather and you. I'd love to see pictures of Mom and Uncle Paul when they were growing up." I glanced around the room. Despite the space available on the desk, the long fireplace mantel, and walls of shelves, there wasn't a family photograph in sight.

"I don't like to display photographs," she said.

"Oh. Well, do you have some picture albums?"

"No."

"How come?" I asked.

"I don't approve of taking pictures of ourselves. It's vain. It glorifies our own image."

I frowned. "It also allows us to remember the people we loved."

Out of the corner of my eye, I saw Matt turn his head slightly.

"You mentioned my cousin," I said. "Does he visit Wisteria often?"

Her eyes flicked sideways, watching Matt. "He lives here."

"Oh, good! Will he be here for dinner?"

I caught the look of amusement in her eyes. "Yes."

"What's he like?"

A sly smile lit the corners of her mouth, as if she were enjoying the game. "You'll have to decide for yourself, Megan."

"Good point. It's not fair to judge people before you actually meet them."

The pleasure she took in our rude standoff convinced me to put an end to it. I rose and walked over to my cousin. "Just so I don't misinterpret things," I said, "I want to know, are you shy or a snob?"

He carefully closed the book and set it back on its shelf, so I got a good look at his profile, a tanned face that was too strongly cut to be described as "cute." His hair was brown and thick.

When he finally turned to me, I was ready to glare back and treat him to what my brothers call "the hot coals." But his eyes took me by surprise. They were dark and beautiful, fathoms deep, like a river on a moonless night. Now I knew why three girls were riding around with him in his Jeep.

We both took a step back. His intense gaze made me unsteady. "I'm Megan," I said, anchoring my hands in my pockets so I wouldn't twist my hair.

"Matt."

He kept staring at me. I waited for him to say more, but he didn't. I wished he was either less good-looking or less of a jerk. I'd rather not be drawn to rude and arrogant guys. Until now, I hadn't been.

"Nice to meet you," I told him.

He nodded, then turned and walked past me to pick up his backpack. "Are we eating at six, Grandmother?"

"As always," she replied.

Apparently our little family reunion was over. "May I go for a walk before dinner?" I asked. "I'd like to look around."

"Keep the house in view," Grandmother warned. "We don't want to have to search for you."

"Would anybody like to come with me?" I added, giving friendliness another try. Maybe Matt would behave better when Grandmother wasn't around.

"No." Her reply was blunt, but it was more of a response than I got from my cousin, who left the room silently.

"Sorry, Matt," I called. "I didn't hear your answer."

He turned back in the hall, a flash of annoyance in his eyes. "No. No, thank you."

I shrugged, wishing it was as easy to toss off the strange attraction I felt toward him.

After promising Grandmother I wouldn't get lost, I headed outside. I made a circle of the house, awed by the expanse of lawn and even more, the tall trees. I found the herb garden, which fit neatly into the L-shape created by the main house and back wing. The brush of my fingers against the plants shook loose a dozen delicious smells. When I exited through the picket gate, I saw what appeared to be another garden, surrounded by a red brick wall with creamy roses tumbling over it. I hadn't noticed it when Ginny drove in, for it was on the far side of the circular drive and I had been focusing on the house. Curious, I strode toward it.

As I got closer, I could see that it was a cemetery, probably a family burial plot. I opened the wrought-iron gate and stepped inside. Some of the gravestones were extremely old, round-shouldered, and leaning forward as if they were tired, their names and dates no longer readable. There were new markers made of shiny granite and I walked over to look at them.

Thomas Barnes, I read. My mother's father. I touched his stone lightly, then turned to the marker next to his. It was fancier, with roses carved into it. *Avril Scarborough.* The name echoed in my mind, as if someone had spoken it from the end of a very long hall. I read her dates, then drew back. I did the math again: She was just sixteen when she died—she was my age.

The grave gave me an eerie feeling. I didn't want to touch her stone. I turned, suddenly compelled to get out of there. As I left I glanced toward the house. The lowering sun flared off the panes of glass; still, I noticed it, the movement of someone stepping back from a second-floor window, as if trying not to be seen. After a moment I realized the person had been watching me from my bedroom. I walked quickly toward the house, but the reflected light made it impossible to see in.

A vague uneasiness seeped into me. Since my arrival, neither Grandmother nor Matt seemed interested in getting to know me. But obviously, someone was interested enough to keep an eye on me.

three

I returned to the house forty minutes later, feeling a million times better, full of the clear blue and gold light of the river and setting sun. I entered by way of the herb garden, walking up onto a covered porch and opening a door that led into the back hall. The small hall, which ran under the stairs, connected the back wing with the center hall of the main house. It had service doors to the dining room and library, and steps leading down to the back wing.

There I found Grandmother in a kitchen with a huge open hearth. An old stove sat halfway inside the blackened fireplace. She stood next to it, stirring something in a pot.

"So you found your way back," she said.

"Yes. I saw the river. It's awesome."

"Then you must not have kept the house in sight,"

Grandmother observed shrewdly. "You cannot see it from any place along the riverbank, not this time of year."

"I, uh, guess I did lose sight of the chimneys. But I have a pretty good sense of direction."

She didn't reply.

"Shall I set the table?" I offered.

"It's set."

So we were eating in the dining room with all those appetizing paintings of dying deer and fox.

"You may carry out the meat and biscuits. The rest will get cold if Matt— Well, it's about time," she told him as he came through the door.

"It's three minutes to six," he replied mildly, then joined her at the stove and began dishing out the greens. I may as well have been a kitchen stool he walked past.

I carried out the platter of meat, then biscuits. He and Grandmother brought the soup and green beans. Grandmother sat at the head of the table with Matt at her right, which left me the seat across from him. As luck would have it, I was also across from the goriest deer of the hunting series.

"We always pray first," Grandmother said as I pulled up my chair.

She folded her hands, resting them on the edge of the table, so I did the same. Matt stared down at his plate.

"Dear Lord," Grandmother began, "forgive us our trespasses this day. Though we lie with our lips and our hearts, call us back to your truth, and grant us mercy rather than the justice we deserve. Amen."

It was the gloomiest dinner prayer I'd ever heard. "Maybe we should give thanks, too," I suggested, "as long as we're praying before a meal."

Matt glanced up.

"You may pray however you like on your own," Grandmother replied, then handed me the ham. "I am relieved to see your parents didn't bring you up to be a complete heathen, though, no doubt, they've passed on some kooky ideas."

"No doubt," I said cheerfully. She wasn't going to drag me and them down. I took a little of the meat, more of the green beans, and one very hard biscuit. A bowl of thick soup was dished out for me.

What appeared to be ham was so salty I could hardly swallow it. It was as if someone had glued fake bacon bits together, then sliced them ultra thin. "What do you call this kind of meat?" I asked.

"Smithfield ham," said Grandmother. "It's a tradition."

I took a long drink of water, ate another mouthful, then bit into a rock-hard biscuit.

"Those are beaten biscuits," Grandmother told me. "Another tradition."

Some of that traditional airplane food I'd turned down was looking pretty good now. I sampled the green beans, then gobbled them up.

"Try your stew," Grandmother ordered.

I pulled the bowl closer and spooned lumps of grayish-white stuff.

"They're not raw," Matt said, "not when they're in the stew."

"What's not raw?" I asked, setting down my spoon.

"The oysters."

I ate one mouthful. It was the slimiest seafood I'd ever tasted, swimming in heavy cream. "May I have the green beans, please?"

"You're not a vegetarian, are you?" Grandmother asked. "I refuse to feed you if you are."

"I'm trying a little of everything, Grandmother," I replied patiently, "but I have always liked green beans." I *used* to like biscuits, I thought, taking another bite of the hard, flat thing.

"It would be just like her parents to raise her as an animal rights extremist," Grandmother said to Matt. "The two of them have always had strange ideas."

It annoyed me to be referred to in the third person, and it hurt to hear my parents put down, but I kept my cool.

"Dad doesn't like hunting," I admitted, "which isn't real surprising since he's a vet. But as you know, Grandmother, his father was an Eastern Shore farmer. Dad was raised on meat and still eats it."

"It's unnatural to avoid meat," she went on.

"Look," I exclaimed, frustrated, "I am *not* a vegetarian! Though the paintings in this room are pushing me in that direction."

Matt's eyes flicked around the room, then came back to me. His dark gaze was unreadable, but at least he'd given up the pretension of not seeing me.

"So what is your mother up in arms about these days?" Grandmother asked. "Migrant workers, I bet."

She knew Mom better than I thought. Two letters on migrant living conditions had been sent to senators last week.

To Matt, Grandmother said, "Carolyn marched for integration, raising taxes for education, luxury condos for chickens—for everything but common sense."

"That's an exaggeration," I countered. "For the chickens she supported two-bedroom apartments."

Matt's mouth twitched, but he remained silent. Grandmother grimly ate her ham and biscuits. Obviously, she had no sense of humor, which meant I wasn't going to be able to joke my way out of an argument.

"College ruined her," Grandmother went on. "It made her a sloppy thinker."

"Mom says that when she arrived at college she found out how narrow-minded she was."

Grandmother laid down her fork. "There was nothing narrow about Carolyn's mind. When she left my house she saw the world clearly and knew right from wrong. After four years away she became hopelessly muddled."

"It is easy to see clearly, when all you see are black and white," I argued, "when you believe that everything has to be one or the other. But it doesn't."

"What is clear to me is that you weren't raised with manners," Grandmother countered, her eyes glittering. She didn't like me, but she liked conflict. "You weren't taught respect for your elders."

"I was. But I don't fake well, and despite what

Mom and Dad say, I don't respect people who don't respect others."

A long silence followed. I chewed and listened to the clink of silverware.

At last Matt pushed back his chair. "I'm going to a movie tonight. Alex is picking me up."

"What movie?" Grandmother asked.

"*Sheer Blue.* It just opened at the theater on High Street."

"That film got a great review in the Tucson paper," I said. "I've been wanting to see it." Maybe he'd take the hint and ask me along. I was eager to be with kids my own age. "The chase sequence is supposed to be fantastic," I added.

"That's what everyone says," he replied. "I'll be home by one o'clock," he told Grandmother, then rose and picked up his dishes.

I wasn't going to be invited.

"You mean twelve-thirty," Grandmother told him. "Who's going besides Alex?"

"Kristy, Amanda, and Kate."

"Oh, the girls you were studying with today," I ventured casually.

He turned around, surprised.

"It's just Alex that he studies with," Grandmother informed me.

"Really?"

Matt gave me a look, which translated into something like *drop dead,* then left.

I sat sipping water, waiting for Grandmother to finish her meal. When she pushed back her chair, I did the same. "Do you have any special instructions for washing dishes?" I asked.

"We each do our own."

"I'll do yours," I offered. "You did the cooking."

"Nancy does the cooking," she corrected me.

"Well, I'm still glad to do them for you."

But, as she said, we each did our own. Grandmother could not bend in any of her ways.

When the kitchen was cleaned up, she told me it was her custom to read in the evening. I could sit in the library with her, as long as I did not talk or listen to music. Her invitation didn't give me warm and cozy feelings. And I doubted she'd approve of the book I'd picked up at the airport: The cover showed a woman with a torn dress and half-bared breasts running from a big house on a stormy night.

As it turned out, sitting inside a cozy circle of lamplight on the high four-poster bed, with the dense night falling around Grandmother's house, was the perfect way to read a gothic romance. When I heard Grandmother come up, I changed into my nightgown but kept turning pages. The face of the deranged housekeeper started to look like Nancy's and the warm-hearted cook spoke with Ginny's voice. The story melted into the events of the day and my eyes closed.

Two hours later I sat straight up, knocking my book off the bed.

I had been dreaming about the house again, playing in the same cozy room with the sloped ceiling and dormer windows. But my old dream had become so clear, so real, I could hardly believe I was awake in a different room. In the dream I had a new toy: a dollhouse that was a miniature of Grandmother's house.

I threw back the quilt and slid off the edge of the bed. The night was brighter than when I'd fallen asleep, the air colder. I pulled a sweatshirt on over my nightgown, then stood at the window that looked down on the herb garden. The late-rising moon silvered the roofs of the back wing, both the shiny tin over the kitchen porch and the duller wood shingles that peaked above each second-floor window. Dormer windows and a sloped roof! Was my playroom in the back wing? Was it real?

I snatched up my purse and dug for my key chain. It had a penlight anchoring it which, with the moonlight, was bright enough to show my way. I eased open the bedroom door. The hall was lit dimly by a lamp on a side table. All the doors were shut, just as they had been earlier in the day.

I glanced back at my alarm clock: 11:59. I doubted Matt would be home before curfew. I slipped down the wide stairway, hurrying past the grandfather clock. In the shadows it seemed like another person, standing stiff and tall on the landing, watching me with disapproval. Just as I reached the bottom of the steps, it began its long toll of twelve.

A lit wall sconce in the lower hall guided me through the door that led into the back hall. I passed the service entrances to the dining room and library and tiptoed down the steps to the rear wing. I walked through the kitchen and opened a door next to the big hearth, then followed a hall that ended at a corner stair.

As I reached the stair, the sound of an engine caught my attention. Matt was being dropped off. I quickly climbed the narrow, triangular steps.

The room at the top had a low, sloping roof, peaked in the middle, with dormer windows on each side, just as in my dream. But it was empty. I played my penlight over the walls. Its beam flashed off a bright object, a knob. I outlined the rectangle of a built-in cupboard, then walked over and opened it.

Something ran across my feet. I jammed my hand in my mouth to keep from screaming, and then to silence my laughter—nervous laughter. The mouse was probably just as rattled. I shone the penlight inside the cupboard and my grip tightened. There it was, the dollhouse, a smaller version of Scarborough House, accurate down to the dormer windows in the back wing where I was standing.

I slid the house out of the cupboard and into a pool of moonlight, then knelt before it. There were large hinges on the corners which allowed the entire front to be opened as one panel. I gently pulled it back. Inside was miniature furniture, replicas of that in the real house.

I sat back on my heels, trying to come up with a reasonable explanation for dreaming about something I'd never seen, then seeing it for real. As a little kid, I used to pretend I was going inside the pictures of my books. I'd imagine fairy-tale castles in three dimensions and daydream about living inside them. Among the photos Uncle Paul had sent Mom, I remembered a picture of her Barbie doll. It was possible that the dollhouse was in those photos and that I had imagined going inside it, until it became a house in my dreams.

As for the similarity between this room and my dream room, there were many ways to account for that. The lodge where my family vacationed in Flagstaff had a sloping roof and dormer windows, and I'd always liked the place. It figured that I'd turn it into a playroom inside my dream house.

I closed the front of the dollhouse and slid it back inside the cupboard. When I stood up, I noticed a door that might lead back to my room by an upstairs route, but played it safe and left the way I had come. At the bottom of the narrow stairs I clicked off my penlight and walked noiselessly toward the kitchen. After making sure that Matt wasn't having a late-night snack, I tiptoed through the kitchen and up the steps connecting the wing to the main house. In the back hall I stopped abruptly.

Matt was in the library, sitting at Grandmother's desk, his back to me. He was leaning over a drawer, searching it, opening files and boxes, sifting through contents that I couldn't see. What was he up to?

For a moment I thought of bursting in and asking him, but then I'd have some explaining to do as well. I slipped down the hall and padded upstairs to my room.

four

Saturday morning Matt and I arrived downstairs at the same time, close to ten o'clock. Grandmother greeted me first. "You've wasted a fine morning."

And good morning to you, too, I thought. But it was a new day and I was determined to make it start out well. "I wish I'd gotten up earlier," I said. "I guess I'm still on Arizona time."

She turned to my cousin. "I don't like being left with the chores, Matt."

"What chores, Grandmother?" he asked, then leaned down from the waist in a runner's stretch.

He was wearing shorts and a T-shirt, which showed off the muscled body of a guy who worked out often. Stop looking, Megan, I told myself.

"You live here," Grandmother answered him sharply. "You know what has to be done."

"Yes," he replied, his voice patient, "but what exactly did you need done?"

"My car has to be washed."

"I did it Thursday afternoon, remember?"

"The house gutters must be cleaned."

"I've done most of that. I'll finish up after the football game this afternoon."

"There is raking."

"It would make more sense in another week."

"Is there something I can do?" I asked.

Matt gave me a cool look. I mirrored it, then saw the spark in Grandmother's eye. She enjoyed the fact that we didn't get along.

"I can handle things," he told me.

What *was* his problem? Did he think I was competing for brownie points? He seemed too sure of himself to worry about being anything less than "number one" with her. And even if some of that confidence was an act, he knew how Grandmother felt about adopted children.

As irritated as I was with Matt, I was even more annoyed with myself for continuing to give him chances to be rude. But something defiant in me, something that refused to believe this was the genuine Matt, kept trying.

"Are you going for a run?" I asked.

He nodded.

"Can I go with you?"

He picked up a plastic bottle from the kitchen counter and twisted off the top. "No."

"Why not?"

"I'm doing serious running."

I prickled. "Meaning you don't think I can keep up with you?"

"Maybe you can," he said with a shrug, then took a vitamin.

"Then why not? In twenty-five words or more," I added, tired of his short answers.

He gazed at me with dark brown eyes. "I work hard year-round to keep in shape for lacrosse. I run cross-country, not little loops around a track."

"At home my dad and I do trails through the Catalinas," I told him. "They're low mountains, but next to the Eastern Shore, they look like the Rockies."

He nodded, unimpressed, then opened a different bottle and took another vitamin.

"Tell me," I said, "what kind of supplement do you take to grow an attitude like yours?"

A crack of a smile, just a crack. Then he pushed both bottles toward me. "Help yourself, though I think your attitude's developed enough."

I glanced at the bottles, which contained ordinary vitamins, then sat down at the kitchen table to drink my juice. I wished I had a newspaper to read, something to page through casually while waiting for him to leave. I grabbed a cereal box and studied that until I heard the screen door bang shut. Out of the corner of my eye I saw Grandmother mark a page in her Bible, then put it on a shelf by the window.

She returned to the table, resting her hands on the

back of a chair. "You're not at all like your mother."

I glanced up, surprised. What an odd comment from someone who never forgot I wasn't related by birth! "Did you expect me to be?"

"Children learn from the person with whom they live. Even as a teenager, your mother was always sweet-natured and gentle with people. She never had a harsh comment for anyone."

"Still doesn't," I said, setting aside the cereal box.

"So where did you get that sharp tongue?" Grandmother asked.

I sighed and stood up. "Don't know. Where did your child get her gentleness?"

I went for a run by myself that morning, following Scarborough Road away from town, passing field after field of harvested corn. I knew better than to expect an invitation to the football game that afternoon. After a long shower and a quick brunch, I asked Grandmother if she wanted to do some shopping in town. She informed me that she only mixed with "the riffraff" when absolutely necessary.

"I shall tell Matt to drop you off," she added.

"Thanks, but I can get there myself."

I figured it was only a twenty-minute walk to the stores on High Street, and I was too proud to accept any ride she had commanded.

In the early afternoon I crossed the bridge over Wist Creek. When I turned onto High Street, I saw a sign advertising "Sidewalk Saturday." About four blocks from the harbor, the shopping district turned into one long sale. Paperbacks were piled in wheelbarrows by the steps of Urspruch's Books. Mobiles and wind chimes dangled from the sycamore tree in front of Faye's Gallery. Teague's Antiques had transformed its patch of bricks into a Victorian parlor with chairs and a sofa. Groups of people strolled in and out of the small shops, some of the crowd walking in the street. Cars crept along, apparently used to this weekend style of life.

When I arrived at Yesterdaze, Ginny barely had time to say hello. Her shop clerk had gone home ill, which left Ginny trying to guide shoppers and cover the register.

"Want some help?" I asked. "I work at Dad's animal hospital. I know how to count change and do credit card purchases."

"Oh, honey, it's your vacation."

"But I'd like to," I told her. "Matt doesn't want to hang out with me. Grandmother doesn't want to hang out with anyone. This would give me something to do."

Ginny played with the amber beads around her neck. "Well, I could sure use a hand," she admitted, her eyes darting after a customer. "You're on."

Wearing a work apron embroidered with the shop's name, armed with credit forms and a money box, I took my place at a table outside. I bagged and boxed. I read price tags and squinted at driver's licenses, copying their numbers onto checks. Some customers were locals, but more were visitors, many from Baltimore and Philadelphia. I enjoyed watching the parade of people and listening to the conversations around me. I learned that shoppers are not as easy to deal with as dogs and cats.

A senior citizen with salon-molded hair argued with Ginny for selling a jacket she had asked Ginny to hold over two months ago. Her nurse companion, a heavyset woman, forty-something, picked through the lace handkerchiefs on the table next to me. "She'll go on like this for another five minutes," said the aide. "Maybe ten. We've argued our way down two blocks of High Street. Always do."

"Sounds like you don't have an easy job," I replied sympathetically.

She shrugged. "Easier than the last one. Pay's better too. Mrs. Barnes thinks it's still 1950."

I looked up from the roll of quarters I had just cracked open. "Mrs. Barnes?"

"Out Scarborough House." The woman kept wrinkling her nose and sniffling, while looking at the elegant handkerchiefs. I was afraid she was going to use one.

"Guess you're not from these parts," she said.

"I, uh, just arrived."

"Well, let me put it this way. Mrs. Barnes makes *her*"—she gestured toward the older woman—"seem like a saint to live with. As for that spooky old house on the Wist, where she'll let you board 'cause she's paying you peanuts, well, I wouldn't live there for any amount of money."

"How come?" I asked, curious.

"It's haunted."

My eyes widened. The woman saw she had an interested audience.

"My sister warned me," she chattered on. "Said it wasn't just the house. It was the family. None of them Scarboroughs was quite right in the head. That's why Mrs. Barnes's daughter ran off like she did. She had to get away."

"From what?"

"Avril Scarborough, I suppose."

I recognized the name from the gravestone.

"She was murdered, you know."

"Murdered!" I repeated with disbelief.

The woman's head bobbed. "The family covered it up. Said it was an accident. It wasn't."

"How do you know it wasn't?" I asked.

"I've seen the ghost. In the rear wing, the room above the kitchen, the only night I stayed there. Say what you want, but happy dead folks don't come back to haunt."

"Alice," the older woman hissed. "I'm ready to go."

"Never asks if *I'm* ready," Alice muttered to me, then stepped forward to take the woman's arm and guide her down the street.

I stared after them. My mother would have told me if someone in her family had been murdered. It's just gossip compounded by Alice's imagination, I thought.

For the next hour we were extremely busy. Still, as I ran my finger down a tax table and stuffed tissue in boxes, I found myself wondering what could have spawned Alice's story. Small-town boredom? Jealousy of a family that had more money than others? Or was there a suspicious event that could be interpreted that way?

I became so lost in thought, I didn't hear what a customer had just said to me. "I'm sorry. What?"

The red-haired girl gazed back at me with wide, clear eyes and smiled a little. "I didn't say anything."

I was certain she had, but perhaps it was the blond girl who had stopped with two friends to sort through items on our sidewalk tables. She looked like the passenger I'd seen in the front seat of Matt's Jeep yesterday. Her two friends echoed whatever opinion she had. She liked the beaded purses, so they liked the beaded purses. She thought the jewelry was for old ladies, so they thought the jewelry was for old ladies.

I noticed that the redhead looked up at the girls once or twice, as if to say hello, but they didn't acknowledge her. Snobs, I thought. She seemed used to it and went back to her own browsing, lifting up a silver chain that dangled a clear blue stone. The gem had the same mystical look as her eyes.

"Try it on," I told her. "There's a mirror inside the store."

She quickly put it down. "I can't buy it."

"So? Doesn't mean you can't try it on."

She looked at me uncertainly, then smiled, picked up the pendant, and went inside.

When I turned to a woman waiting to buy a lace

collar, I saw the two echoes watching me, but the blond quickly got their attention with a comment about the shop's ugly old jewelry. I focused on finding my customer the right-size box, pulling out a flat piece of cardboard, then fitting the tabs into their slots.

"Matt! Hey, Matt!" the blond called out, and I glanced up.

My cousin and three other guys strode toward her and her friends.

So that's what you look like when you smile, I thought. It was a terrific smile, I noted grudgingly, then lined my customer's box with tissue.

"Hi, Kristy," he greeted the blond. "Amanda, Kate."

"We missed you," Kristy said to him. "We didn't see you at the game."

"Oh, I think you did," he replied lightly. "I was sitting with Charles, remember?"

"Your sports buddy." I heard the sneer in her voice; raising my head, I saw it on her face.

"He's my teammate," Matt said, still smiling. "You're always sitting with your teammates," he added, nodding at the echoes.

Boy, did he know how to flirt with those eyes! The girls on either side of her giggled.

"They're friends," she told him, in a fake, quarreling voice. "We don't play a sport."

"Partying," he said. "Isn't that one?"

They all laughed.

I stamped my customer's check with an irritated

thump. Why was he so flirty and charming to some people and such a jerk to me? I handed the package to my customer.

"Thanks very much. Come again," I said quietly.

Apparently, not quietly enough. I was turning my George Washingtons face up, counting the singles, when I realized that Matt's group of friends had stopped talking. I looked up to see him staring at me.

"What are you doing here?" he asked. He sounded as if he'd caught me trespassing.

"Working. You got a problem with that?"

The blond-haired guy next to Matt glanced sideways at him and smiled.

"You're supposed to be visiting Grandmother," he told me.

"I don't remember clearing my schedule with you."

His friend laughed out loud, which annoyed Matt.

"In fact," I added, "I don't remember *you* showing an interest in anything I was doing."

Everyone but the grinning guy looked uncomfortable. Kristy moved closer to my cousin. "Who is she?"

I prickled at her tone.

"Megan, my cousin, sort of," Matt replied.

"What do you mean by sort of?" asked the smiling guy.

"Matt's father is my uncle, sort of," I said.

The guy looked from Matt to me. There was a brightness in his blue eyes, a spark of laughter. I liked him immediately. "So, who are you?" I asked bluntly.

"Alex Rodowsky." He held out his right hand.

"Your sort-of cousin's friend. I hope he's not grumpy like this at home."

"He is."

Matt scowled.

"When he starts it with me," Alex said, "I just ignore him."

"Is he like this a lot?" I asked. "How long does he stay this way?"

What a scowl!

"Don't you know? You're his cousin," Alex pointed out.

"We met for the first time yesterday. Though Matt has disliked me long before that."

Alex looked puzzled.

I heard Matt suck in his breath and let it out slowly. "Maybe we should talk at home, Megan."

"Why, that would be a nice change!"

He didn't reply.

"Megan?" Ginny called through the door. "Can you give me twenty singles?"

"Be right in," I said, banding the stack of bills I had just counted.

Matt's friends drifted off. The way the girls bent their heads together, I figured they were discussing me. I picked up the cash box to carry inside, but Ginny met me at the door. "Thanks, honey. I don't know what I'd do without you."

I returned to my post in time to see Alex pull Matt back from the departing group.

"What's this sort-of cousin stuff?" he asked, not

bothering to keep his voice down, perhaps thinking I was inside. "Is she or isn't she?"

"Legally she is, but not really," Matt replied. "She's adopted."

"Which means you can date her," Alex said. "Are you interested?"

"No," Matt answered quickly.

"Good. I am."

"She's got a mouth," my cousin warned.

His friend shrugged. "Makes it easier to kiss."

Matt must have made a strange face because Alex laughed at him, then walked off to join the others. Matt glanced back over his shoulder. His jaw dropped a little when he realized I was standing there.

I turned away just as the redhead was coming from inside the shop.

"Want to see how it looks?" she asked, smiling shyly. "Miss Ginny told me to try these earrings with it. The stone is aquamarine."

"I knew it would look great on you!"

She touched the stone lightly, then reluctantly reached back for the clasp.

"Too much?"

"Yes," she said, handing it to me.

I glanced at the tag. "Whoa! That's a lot of Big Macs."

I put it back in the velvet case and she set the earrings next to it.

"I'm Sophie. Sophie Quinn."

"Megan Tilby," I told her.

"Nice to meet you. I, uh, was standing at the door when Matt was talking to Alex," Sophie said. "Matt's your cousin?"

"Legally." Darn, I thought; now I'm making that distinction. "I'm visiting for two weeks."

"I hope you have a real good time. I probably shouldn't ask this, but has Matt told you anything about the girls at school and, well, who he likes?"

I started to laugh at the thought of him confiding in me, then stifled it, realizing Sophie might have a crush on him. "Why? Are you interested in him?"

She blushed a little. "Every girl in the senior class is interested in him," she told me. "And Matt never lets on who he really likes, which makes all the girls crazy."

I shook my head. "Sorry, I don't have a clue. I don't really know him."

Sophie nodded. "I guess he's just one of those people who gets along with everyone."

Nearly everyone, I thought.

five

At four o'clock Ginny told me to take a break and sent me to Tea Leaves with some money. Figuring that tonight's dinner would be leftovers from last night's, I splurged and got a piece of chocolate cheesecake.

The café was a comfortable place with a worn tile floor and painted tables and chairs, none of the sets matching. At the back was a long glass case filled with bakery items, as well as a refrigerator case with yogurt and salads. A lady with fuzzy hair and a man who looked like a fifty-year-old Pillsbury Doughboy waited on customers. The man had a round, pleasant face that creased easily into a smile. He called many of the customers by name.

I carried my dessert to a table by the bay window, glad for a chance to sit down. There was a sign in the window, its letters faded but readable: Fortunes Told

Here. Well, I didn't need a psychic to tell me I was headed for two tough weeks. Why did Matt dislike me so much? I wondered. I had never had trouble making friends. It was as if he'd made up his mind about me before we'd met.

I took a forkful of cheesecake, then another. Stop trying to figure Matt out, I told myself. He's a jerk.

"Everything okay?"

The round-faced man had come from behind the counter to wipe down tables. "If you don't like your selection, help yourself to something else."

I realized I must have been frowning.

"Whatever you want. On the house," he added.

"Oh, no!" I said quickly. "It's the best cheesecake I've ever had."

He smiled. "And you know, it doesn't have a single calorie—as long as you just look at it." He laughed at his own joke and I laughed with him. "You're not one of my regulars," he observed. "Just visiting for the day?"

"For a couple weeks," I replied. "I'm staying with my grandmother."

"And who might that be?"

"Helen Barnes."

He stopped wiping a table and gazed at me with surprise. I readied myself for another strange Scarborough story, but as it turned out, I was the cause for amazement.

"I didn't know she had a granddaughter."

"And two grandsons," I said. "I mean in addition to Matt. I have two younger brothers."

He straightened up. "Really! So you all must be Carolyn's children."

"Carolyn and Kent Tilby." I worked hard to keep my voice from sounding brittle. It wasn't this man's fault that Grandmother never mentioned us.

"The Tilbys. They had a farm up Oyster Creek. But they passed away."

I nodded.

"Carolyn and Kent hooked up in college. I remember now. I just didn't know they had kids. Well, welcome. It's a pleasure to have you. Tell your folks Jamie says hi. Riley's the last name, though nobody calls me anything but Jamie." He held out a damp hand and I shook it. "Back when they knew me, my father ran this place, and I had dreams bigger than puff pastry. But it turned out baking is what I do well," he added.

"Really well," I agreed, sliding another bite of cheesecake into my mouth. "Who does the fortune-telling?"

"My mother." He glanced toward the window. "I should get rid of that sign. She's getting too old. Of course she's always happy to do a reading for a local. How about it? I'm sure Mama would be interested to meet you," he added before I could refuse. "She's known the Scarboroughs all her life. When she was a teenager, she worked for them, even lived at the house for a while."

"She did?" His mother would probably know if there was anything to Alice's story. "I'd love to have my fortune told."

"I'll call upstairs and ask if she's free. We live right above here," he added, pointing to the stairway that ran up the side wall of the cafe. "Makes it an easy commute to work."

I smiled. "Thanks."

After finishing the cheesecake, I walked over to the bakery case to buy some pastries for Ginny and muffins for myself. I had just made my final selection when I heard Jamie's voice behind me: "Here she is, Mama."

I turned around. Mrs. Riley was a small woman with dark brown hair, my grandmother's age or older.

"Mama, this is Megan Tilby."

"Hi, Mrs. Riley."

She looked at me but didn't speak.

"This is Mrs. Barnes's granddaughter," Jamie added a moment later. "Carolyn and Kent's girl," he said, as if trying to nudge a response from her.

But she just stared at me. The hair dye she used made her face look pale. The lines around her mouth were deep.

"Hi," I said again, a little louder this time, in case she had trouble hearing. "It's nice to meet you."

I held out my hand. She didn't take it.

"Mama?" Jamie seemed as puzzled as I. "This is the young lady who wants her fortune told."

She turned on him, her eyes blazing. "You were a fool to say I'd do it. I will not look into the cards for her." Then she stalked across the room and up the steps, moving quickly for an old woman.

Jamie's face turned red with embarrassment. "I–I don't know what to say," he stammered. "I'm very sorry, Megan. She's not always agreeable, and hasn't been that well lately, but I didn't expect this."

"Don't worry about it," I assured him. "She's probably just tired. I'll come back another time."

He nodded, but still seemed concerned, whether for her feelings or mine, I wasn't sure.

"Really," I said, "it's no big deal."

I paid for my purchases and left, feeling like that woman in mythology–the one who had snakes for hair–Medusa. One look at me, and some people turned to stone.

Grandmother gave me permission to eat with Ginny that evening. We locked up the shop about six-thirty and went out to dinner. During the meal, Ginny asked if I'd be interested in filling in for her sick employee starting Monday. I jumped at the chance. I loved all the activity of High Street and was relieved that someone in Wisteria wanted me around.

By the time I got home that evening, Matt had left for a school dance. I joined Grandmother in the library, eager to tell her what and who I had seen in town. But she responded so negatively to the first few things I told her, I gave up well before I got to the strange Mrs. Riley.

I crawled into bed that night exhausted. Even so, I tossed and turned. The tall clock on the stair landing chimed every quarter hour, telling me the amount of rest I didn't get. A cold front was passing through. It rattled shutters and windowpanes and sent wind diving down the house's chimneys. My bedroom door shook so hard it sounded as if someone was trying to get in. I got up and latched it firmly. Finally I drifted into sleep.

It was some time later, when the rough weather had settled down to an eerie silence, that I again became aware of my surroundings. The voice awakened me.

"My name is Avril."

My eyes flew open and I glanced around the room. The whisper lacked the warmth of a human voice. I wasn't sure if it was inside my head or out. I lay as still as possible, listening, my skin prickling.

"My name is Avril."

I sat up and pulled the quilt around me. My skin felt as if it were crawling off my bones. "Who's there?"

Silence.

I gazed at the bedroom door, waiting for something to happen, the knob to turn, the whisperer to whisper again. My breath felt trapped inside my chest, my heart pounded in my ears.

You've got a choice, I told myself. You can cower here for the rest of the night, or you can prove that it was nothing but a voice in a dream, your imagination playing tricks.

I climbed out of bed, then tiptoed to the door. Taking a deep breath, I cracked it slowly, then yanked it wide open.

No one. Nothing. Just the tick tock tick of the big clock. I walked quietly into the hall. The clock's white face showed a few minutes after one.

Matt's door was closed, as was Grandmother's— which didn't mean they were actually in their rooms. With the house's interconnecting chimneys and old heating system, it would be easy enough to whisper something downstairs so it could be heard upstairs. Was Matt having a little fun with me?

I walked quickly toward the hall window to check for his Jeep; he was home. Still, playing ghost seemed like too much trouble for him. Till now, his way of dealing with me was to ignore me and hope I went away.

I listened for a moment by the door of his room, straining for some hint that he was awake. There was no sound but that of the clock. Giving up, I headed back to my room. As I passed the hall mirror, I glanced at it, then froze.

There, in the antique glass, I saw her, more light than substance, a changing wisp of fog, the shape of a girl. I stared at the mist in the mirror, struggling to understand what I was seeing. Avril? I felt icy cold all over.

I ran for my room and pulled the door closed behind me. It didn't catch. When I reached my bed, I heard the door swing open again, but I was too afraid to look back. Hands shaking, I pulled down my quilt in a rush to get in bed, then gasped with disbelief. She was there! She was lying there in front of me! No, it was *me* I was looking down on. And I was dead! I squeezed shut my eyes and put my hands over my mouth, barely muffling screams that echoed deep within me.

When I opened my eyes again, I was lying in bed, warm and safe beneath my quilt. It was a dream, I told myself, just a scary dream. Then I turned my head on the pillow and saw the door I'd latched earlier standing wide open.

SIX

As soon as I emerged from bed Sunday morning, I felt the draft, a river of icy air flowing between the fireplace and entrance to my room. I hurried across the chilly floorboards to close the door. Memories of last night washed over me.

It was just a dream, I told myself—the whisper, the ghost in the mirror—they were nothing more than a nightmare seeded by what a customer had said. As for the door being open, old houses weren't airtight; it wasn't surprising after a windy night.

I dressed quickly, glad my mother had made me pack a long-sleeved turtleneck and sweater. When I arrived in the kitchen, neither Grandmother nor Matt was around. I made a steaming cup of tea and took it out to the kitchen garden.

The river mist was suffused with early-morning sun-light. In the garden every dew-drenched leaf, from the flat needles of rosemary to the smallest teardrops of thyme, shimmered. I walked to the picket fence that edged the garden, stopping at the gate, gazing toward the family cemetery. From a distance the roses looked like soft pink and white smudges against the brick wall. I thought of the voice from last night. Was it possible—had the girl buried there come up to the house? I shivered.

"Need another sweater?"

I hadn't heard Matt approach. "No, thanks."

"You look cold."

He was wearing a short-sleeved shirt with his jeans. I'd turn into an iceberg before admitting to him I had goose bumps beneath my sweater. "I'm not."

"How did you sleep last night?" he asked.

"Fine. Great."

I could see it in his eyes, he didn't believe me.

"Why wouldn't I?" I asked.

He shrugged. "If you're not used to an old house, it can be a spooky kind of place when the wind kicks up."

He studied my face, and I, in turn, studied his.

"Guess I'm a solid sleeper," I said. "How about you?"

"I'm a light sleeper. I hear just about everything."

Like a girl's muffled scream? I wondered. I took a sip of tea.

"So, did you have a good time last night?" I asked. "I mean at the dance, not afterward." I watched him over the rim of my cup. But if he had been up to something afterward, like whispering in a ghostly voice, he didn't show it.

"No. I've always hated school dances."

"Then why did you go?"

"Everyone expects you to," he replied matter-of-factly.

"Do you always do what others expect?"

One side of his mouth pulled up in that smirky smile of his. "Not always."

"You're right about that. Most people would expect you to be friendly to a cousin you'd just met, or at least polite to a house guest."

He glanced away.

"Listen, Matt, I didn't want to come here."

"Then why did you?"

"Grandmother asked me to," I replied.

"Do you always do what others ask?"

"Not always," I said, giving him the same smirk he had given me a moment ago. "My father talked me into it. And I'm not brownnosing Grandmother—I'm not here for her money, if that's what you're worried about. Dad's hoping I can heal things between Grandmother and Mom. I think he's wrong, but, as it turns out, I'm glad I'm here."

Matt remained silent.

"I believe in making the best of a situation," I added. "Why do you keep trying to make the worst of it?"

He didn't reply, just stared down at my face as if he were searching for something.

"Too bad you have such beautiful eyes."

Seeing him blink, I realized I had said that aloud.

"You have no problem speaking your mind," he replied, those eyes now bright with amusement.

I turned away from him. "Grandmother's standing in the window, waiting for us to come in, and looking annoyed."

I headed toward the porch and Matt followed.

"Good morning, Grandmother," I greeted her as we entered the kitchen.

"Good morning, Megan. Matt, you're up early for Sunday. I heard you come in before midnight last night. Were you ill?"

"No."

"Well, for once, you can get a good start on your studying," she remarked.

He nodded, strode over to the kitchen cupboard, and got out a glass.

She turned to me. "Megan, your mother has written that you're an honor student. Perhaps you can help Matt."

I saw Matt's hand tighten around the glass and I shook my head. "No, he's a year ahead of me."

"But you're taking Advanced Placement courses and getting straight A's," Grandmother insisted.

I looked at her, surprised. Apparently she had more contact with my mother than I'd realized.

"Matt, most definitely, is not getting A's or even B's," she went on.

Why was she comparing us? I doubted it was grandmotherly pride in my achievements.

"He's never been a good student," she continued.

Matt poured juice in his glass, his face expression-less.

"Perhaps you can motivate him," Grandmother added.

This wasn't about motivation, it was a comparison aimed at making him dislike me even more than he already did.

"Thanks for letting me have dinner with Ginny," I said, deliberately changing the subject.

Grandmother nodded and began eating her banana. "She was impressed with the way you handled customers. Matt, did you hear that Megan was offered a job?"

He kept his back to us as he returned the carton of juice to the refrigerator. "I saw her working yesterday."

"Did you know she was asked to continue?"

"That's nice," he replied.

"I have wanted Matt to get a job since last spring."

"Well," I said lightly, "I can't really see him selling purses and lace handkerchiefs."

She didn't smile and wasn't diverted from her goal. "He claims he has enough to handle with athletics and school, and of course his social life. I suppose it's my fault for continuing to give him money."

I wasn't getting into that. And I wasn't going to allow her to play me against him.

"Anyone want a muffin?" I asked, retrieving the bag from the counter where I had left it last night. "They're from Tea Leaves."

Matt didn't reply. Grandmother glanced at the bag, then lapsed into silence, sipping her coffee. Had she said her piece, or was she resting before unloading another round of antagonizing comments?

She washed her dishes, then walked over to the shelf where I had seen her put the Bible the day before. "Where is it?" she asked, turning quickly to us.

"Where's what?" Matt asked casually and dropped a slice of bread in the toaster.

"My Bible."

"It's not on the shelf?" He craned his neck to look around her.

Her eyes bore down on me. "Which of you has taken it?"

"I haven't touched it, Grandmother," I said, surprised by her accusatory tone.

"And you know I never do," Matt added.

"Someone moved it. I put it here last night. It is always here," she insisted.

"Maybe you carried it into another room," I suggested.

"I did not. I know what I've done and what I haven't."

"But everybody misplaces things," I reasoned with her. "I'll look in the library." It was an excuse to get away as much as a desire to help. She seemed bent on raising a fuss this morning, and I didn't want any part of it.

I checked her desk first, then the tabletops and mantel. Matt came in and began searching even more thoroughly, beneath tables and chairs, under a pile of magazines. I returned to the desk and tried to open the drawers, the ones he'd been looking through Friday night.

"They're locked," he said.

"Where's the key?"

"I don't know," he replied. "Some things Grandmother tells no one."

Except you, I thought.

"The Bible wouldn't be in there anyway," he added.

"How would you know, if the desk is locked?"

His eyes met mine steadily. "I've seen the drawers open when she's working. They're full of junk. There's no room for anything else." He turned to survey the shelves of books. "Are you sure you didn't borrow it or put it away for her?"

"I'm sure."

His eyes continued to travel over the volumes of books. "If she put it on one of these shelves, we'll be lucky to find it."

He was acting as if we had a major problem on our hands. "It'll show up sooner or later," I said. "And if it doesn't, she can buy a new one—it's still in print."

He didn't smile. "You look in the music room, I'll search the parlor."

I checked the room thoroughly; nothing but dust had settled there for a long time. I returned to the kitchen, figuring that Grandmother had found the book or decided it was not important.

She spun around when she heard me enter. "It is a sin to steal."

"I know, Grandmother. The Ten Commandments are posted in my bedroom."

She glared at me, then started pacing back and forth.

"We'll find it," I assured her. "Meanwhile, it's Sunday. Is there a church service you like in town? I'd be glad to go with—"

"I don't go to church," she replied shortly. "I refuse to sit among the town hypocrites. As for the ministers these days, they can't tell right from wrong."

Matt returned. "Should I check your bedroom, Grandmother?"

"You should check *Megan's* room," she replied.

I opened my mouth to protest. Her suspicion was insulting. But if a search put me in the clear—"Oh, what the heck, check it," I said.

All three of us climbed the stairs. Matt searched my room, taking too long I thought. Grandmother checked his room. I offered to search hers but was met with a look that could shear steel. I sat on the top step stewing, then got up and walked in circles. When I passed in front of the hall's antique mirror, I saw myself looking angry and on edge.

The two of them returned empty-handed.

"Someone will be punished for this," Grandmother declared.

She sounded absurdly serious.

"Maybe the ghost took it," I suggested.

"We don't have a ghost, Megan. I don't want to hear that kind of nonsense from you."

I was feeling defiant. "Someone named Alice, who used to work here, told me she saw it."

"Alice Scanlon is a liar."

"She said the ghost's name is Avril."

The pupils of Grandmother's eyes were jet black inside their pale blue rims. Matt shook his head, signaling me to keep quiet.

"On my walk Friday I visited the family cemetery and saw Avril's stone. She died young."

"She was the same age as you," Grandmother replied. "And just as sassy."

"How did she die?"

Grandmother looked at me for a long moment, the pupils of her eyes unsteady. "You heartless, rude girl, asking me something like that. You're not part of the family. Why would I tell you?"

"So when people say things, like she was murdered, I know how to correct them."

She turned abruptly, strode into her bedroom, and slammed the door behind her. There was a moment of quiet, then I heard her lock the door.

I looked at my cousin, hoping he could give me a reasonable explanation for her extreme behavior.

"Good job," he said. "Next time you set her off, do it on a day I'm out of the house."

"She's already off," I replied in a hushed voice.

"Yeah, well, if you don't want her over the edge, you'll drop the ghost stuff."

"She overreacts to things," I argued.

"And you won't mention Avril again."

"Why?" I asked, following him downstairs. I caught his arm at the landing. "Tell me why."

"It upsets Grandmother. Avril was her sister and they were very close."

"*Sixty* years ago. She can't still be mourning her. Matt, is Grandmother losing it? Mentally, I mean."

He started down the steps again, ignoring the question.

I caught up with him a second time. "Why do you protect her? When she goes after you, why don't you fight back?"

"There are a lot of things you don't understand."

"No kidding. How about explaining them to me?"

He was silent.

"Couldn't you see what she was doing with that stuff about grades and jobs? She's trying to turn you against me. I don't know why, since you already don't like me. But she's making sure of it. What's eating her?"

For a moment the mask slipped from his face. I could see the uncertainty in him.

"Matt," I said, taking a step toward him.

He jerked away from me, picked up his Jeep keys from the hall table, and strolled toward the door.

"What are you thinking?" I called after him. "What?"

He didn't glance back, didn't break stride. "You should never have come," he said, and left.

seven

grandmother emerged from her room at ten o'clock that morning, no longer obsessed with finding the Bible. She was unhappy because Matt had left the house on his study day, but he knew how to get back on her good side, returning with the Baltimore paper, as well as the Sunday *New York Times* and *Washington Post*. Her fingers smoothed the newspaper with the same pleasure that some women show when touching silk. Anyone peeking in the library door right then would have thought she was a perfectly normal grandmother.

"Are you calling your mother today?" she asked me.

"I was thinking about e-mailing my parents. Do you have a computer?"

"Matt has one in his room. You may use that."

"Is that all right with you, Matt?"

Grandmother replied before he did. "I gave him the computer. It is all right with me."

Still, I waited for my cousin's response.

"It's on," he said, which I took as permission and headed upstairs.

Matt's room was neater than I thought it would be, with just a few pretzels crunched into the rug and a small pile of clothes thrown onto a chair. Two pictures sat on a shelf above his desk. In one several lacrosse players wearing helmets and holding sticks grinned back at the camera. I thought Matt was the player on the end. The second photo was of a little boy and a big dog. I knew by the eyes that the child was Matt, but the sweetness of his expression surprised me. His arms were wrapped so lovingly around the dog, a golden retriever that looked old and patient, I got a lump in my throat.

I finally sat down, called up my e-mail account, and began to type. I had decided writing would be better than calling because I could choose what to say and what to leave out. There was no point in upsetting my mother by telling her about Grandmother's eccentric behavior. And I didn't want to be overheard when I asked about Aunt Avril and the dollhouse.

I was finishing the letter when I heard voices in the hall. Matt entered the room with his friend, Alex.

"Almost done?" he asked.

"Just signing off," I told him.

Alex dropped down in the chair next to the desk. "Hi, Megan. I was hoping you'd be here."

I smiled. "Hi! Matt didn't tell me you were coming over."

Alex stretched his long legs out in front of him. "You must have figured out by now that if you want to know anything, you have to pry it out of Matt."

My cousin, standing behind Alex's chair, grimaced slightly.

"We study together every Sunday," Alex added. "Want to hang out with us?"

"No," Matt said.

Alex glanced over his shoulder and laughed. "I wasn't asking you."

"Even so—" Matt began.

I interrupted: "You must have figured out by now, I'm not one of Matt's favorite people."

"Yeah?" Alex replied, his dark blue eyes sparkling. "Why?"

I shrugged. "Let me know if he tells you first."

Matt stood silently with his hands on his hips.

"Don't worry about it," Alex said. "Sometimes he's just strange."

I laughed. Matt shifted his weight from foot to foot.

"Are you a lacrosse player, too?" I asked Alex, pointing to the photograph. "Are you one of those guys in a helmet?"

"I play lacrosse, but that's not our team." Alex turned to look at my cousin, waiting for him to explain the photo. "Did you forget how to talk, Matt?"

"That's my team at Gilman," Matt said, "the school I went to in Baltimore."

When he fell silent, Alex continued, "Matt and I got to be friends at lacrosse camp, the one Chase College runs every summer. A bunch of guys on our team go to it, so when Matt finally moved here last year, he fit right in. He's the strongest guy on our team and plays awesome defense. He set a school record for assists last season."

"Wow," I said, impressed.

One side of Matt's mouth drew up.

There was no use arguing my sincerity. "Was that your dog, Matt?" I asked, pointing to the other photo.

"Yes."

"What's his name?"

"Homer."

"Homer?" I repeated. "You named him after the Greek writer? The guy who wrote the *Iliad*?"

Alex threw back his head and laughed. "Yeah, and he had a cat named Shakespeare."

I saw the pink creeping up Matt's neck.

"Not exactly," he said. "When I found him, he was hungry and hurt and looked like he needed a home. So I called him Homer."

I felt that strange little lump in my throat again. I carefully took the photo from the shelf and studied it. In grade school I had one special cat who heard all of my secrets and sorrows. This dog had probably listened to a few as well, especially since Matt was the only child of parents who were always fighting.

"There's a lot of chatter in here, and it doesn't sound like schoolwork."

The three of us looked toward the door, where Grandmother stood.

"Then you must not have been listening real hard," Alex told her. "We were just talking about the famous Greek writer, Homer."

"I believe that, and you'll tell me another one," Grandmother replied.

"I heard someone mention Shakespeare," he added.

"Save your lines for your girlfriends, Alex."

To my amazement, she was smiling.

He grinned at her. "My father said to tell you he's still hoping you'll change your mind and let him interview you for his Eastern Shore history."

"Your father will be hoping till Doomsday, at which point no one will be interested."

Alex laughed. "He wants one of the professors in his department to have a look at the old mill."

"I don't know why your father persists in thinking of me as anything but a grouchy old woman, who means no when she says no."

"It's the newspapers," Alex replied. "You're the only person in town who reads as many newspapers and magazines as he does. No matter what I tell him about you, he's convinced you're not all bad."

Grandmother clucked.

She liked this teasing, I realized. In some ways she was like me, always ready with a comeback, enjoying the give and take. *Except* she didn't enjoy it with me.

"It's time to get to work," she said, her voice turning prim, like a girl who'd decided her flirting had gone on too long. "I want to hear lessons," she said as she exited the room.

Matt tossed several notebooks on his desk.

"Golden retrievers are terrific dogs," I remarked, looking again at the picture in my hands. "How long did you have him?"

"Two years."

"What happened?"

"When we moved out, my mother said I had to get rid of him."

First his parents separated, then his mother got rid of his dog? "That's terrible! Homer was yours."

"It was no big deal," he replied, shrugging it off.

"Faker," I said softly.

I saw a flicker of emotion in his eyes, then he reached for the picture. "We should put this back." He set it gently on the shelf.

"Well, thanks for the use of your computer."

"Sure." His voice was quieter than usual.

"Hope I'll see you around, Megan," Alex said.

"Yeah, me, too," I replied, pretty certain I wouldn't, not if he hung out with Matt.

"When do you turn on the heat?" I asked, soaking my hands in the hot dishwater, wishing the rest of me felt as warm. I had taken a walk before dinner and come back chilled. The cold fried chicken and potato salad hadn't warmed me up any.

"November," Matt answered, "if we're lucky. It's a big house to heat and Grandmother watches her money."

I didn't complain further, not wanting to seem like a wimp from the sunny Southwest. But having left behind ninety-degree days, I was freezing when the temperature plummeted to the low fifties. The dampness here added a raw edge that went right through my bones.

Drying my hands, I went upstairs to put on a heavy sweater, then joined Grandmother in the library for an evening of reading the newspaper. A few minutes later, Matt came in carrying several logs.

"What are you doing?" Grandmother asked him.

"Building a fire."

She studied him for a moment, then looked at me with my turtleneck yanked up to my ears and my sweater sleeves down to my knuckles. "How thoughtful."

The sarcasm in her voice made me reluctant to thank Matt in front of her. Besides, Grandmother was wearing a thick sweater, too; maybe he was doing this for her.

Matt built the fire, arranging the logs and stacking the kindling in a quiet, methodical way. He had rolled up his sleeves so I could see the muscles in his forearms. His hands were large, with the wide palms and long, strong fingers of an athlete. I wondered what it would be like to hold hands with him, then quickly squelched that thought.

He struck a match. As soon as it was dropped on the crumpled newspaper, I was down on the floor, close to the hearth. He dropped in another match. A piece of newspaper flared up, then collapsed quickly into ash. Small sticks caught and made crackling noises. Big sticks burned and the outside of a heavy log began to char.

Matt turned to me. "If you keep sighing like that, you're going to blow out the fire."

I covered my mouth with my hand. A smile touched the corners of his lips.

"I love fires," I said.

"No kidding." Maybe it was the hissing log that made his words seem softer.

I suddenly became aware of Grandmother observing us with a sour look on her face. I sat back quickly and spread the newspaper on the bricks in front of me, then lay on my stomach and began to read. The golden light flickered over the paper. I could feel its warmth on my face.

Matt found the sports page and lay on his stomach about a foot away from me. I didn't look back at Grandmother, figuring we would have heard if she had any objections to our reading on the floor. I was more relaxed than I'd been since leaving home. Soon the print in front of me got blurry and my head felt too heavy to hold up.

I don't know how long I slept, probably just a few minutes. The sound of a shifting log awakened me. When I opened my eyes I saw that Matt had stopped reading. His face was turned toward me, his eyes, like dark embers, watching me.

Look away, I thought. Turn away now before it's too late.

But I couldn't. Gazing back into his eyes, I felt something stir inside me, some feeling so deep, so secret, my own heart couldn't whisper the words to me.

Grandmother coughed and Matt and I glanced aside at the same time. I sat up and moved over two feet, so I could sit with my back against a chair. Matt poked at the fire.

That's when I noticed it, above Matt's shoulder, on a shelf to the left of the mantel.

"Grandmother, look. Your Bible."

She glanced at me, then her head jerked in the direction that I pointed. Her mouth opened with surprise. She sat still in her chair as if she couldn't believe she was seeing it. I scrambled to my feet, retrieved the Bible, and carried it over to her. When she didn't take it from my hands, I laid it in her lap.

"Which of you wicked children put it there?" she demanded.

Matt and I looked at each other. "Neither," I said after a moment.

"Liar!"

I stepped back. Matt got a guarded look on his face.

Grandmother started paging through the heavy book, then looked up at the gap on the shelf where the Bible had been. The pale blue of her eyes thinned inside a ring of white. "Put something there, Matt. Now!" she cried. "Put it *there!*"

Matt picked up several magazines and stuffed them in the space. "Are you all right?"

Her hands were shaking badly. "I'm looking for Corinthians," she said.

"Can I help?" I asked.

"*You* stay away."

I retreated to a chair.

"I have it," she said, and began to read Paul's famous passage about charity—what love is and isn't. Her voice quivered when she read how all things but love would pass away. Matt stood close to her, his face lined with concern. Despite what he had said before, he must have been worried about her state of mind. It was her intensity, the anger and suspicion with which she spoke, more than what she said, that was frightening.

She looked up suddenly. "Finish it, Matt. Verses eleven and twelve."

"Why don't we finish it later?" he suggested quietly.

"I want to hear it now."

"You know I don't like to read aloud."

"Read it!" She shoved the book in his hands.

He hesitated, then took a deep breath and carried the Bible to her desk. Sitting down in front of the book, he focused on the page for a few moments, marking the place with his finger.

"When I was a . . . a child," he began, "I . . . played–"

"Spake!" she corrected him.

"I spake as a ch-child, I . . . understand–"

"Understood."

"I understood as a child." His face was tense with concentration. "I tough as–"

"Thought!"

"I thought as . . . a child."

I listened with disbelief. Matt could barely read.

"But where I because a name–"

"But when I became a man," Grandmother said in a low, ugly voice.

He nodded and swallowed. "I . . . put . . . away childish thoughts."

"Things. Give it to me, Matt."

"You wanted me to read," he said, his jaw clenched. "I'm going to finish it."

I closed my eyes, wishing I weren't there.

"For no, we see . . . uh–"

"Through a glass darkly," I said softly.

"For now we see through a glass darkly; but the– but then . . . fa-face to face; No I now–" He shook his head and started again. "–Now I know in part; but there–then shall I now–know–ever as also I am known."

The passage was finally over. Matt looked grim and humiliated; I knew anything I said would only make it worse for him.

Anger simmered inside me. I didn't know what made Grandmother act the way she did. It was as if certain things could turn on a switch in her and make her cold and mean. What dark, distorted glass did she look through when she got this way?

I couldn't begin to guess. Only one thing was clear to me: Matt was dyslexic and Grandmother was trying desperately to shame him in front of me.

eight

I awoke Monday morning just as the sky was getting bright. I knew I was at Grandmother's house, but something was different about the pale gray light. It reflected off a ceiling that was too close. My eyes traveled down to the walls. Faded roses, huge as headlights, surrounded me. I wasn't in my room. I sat up quickly and realized the surface beneath me was hard. I'd been sleeping on the floor of a small room that was wallpapered in roses.

I scrambled to my feet and went to a window. Below me was the herb garden and the long tin roof that covered the kitchen porch. I was in the back wing, in the room next to the one with the dormer windows where I had found the dollhouse. The closed door to my right must have led to that room. Opposite from it was an open door that revealed five steps, which rose to the second floor hall of the main house.

I walked slowly around the empty room, trying to remember how I had gotten here. I couldn't recall waking up and moving. Was I sleepwalking? I had done it once or twice as a kid. I struggled to remember last night's dreams, hoping for some clue as to why I had left my room. All I could remember was something round, a circle with bumps or marks on its circumference.

I wondered who had used this room and for what. Perhaps it was a housekeeper's or maid's room. Then I recalled what Alice, the customer at Yesterdaze, had said. "I've seen the ghost. In the rear wing, in the room above the kitchen."

The skin at the back of my neck prickled. Avril? I mouthed her name, afraid to say it aloud, as if I had the power to summon her. Had she been here last night? Had I followed her here?

"Get a grip, Megan," I muttered.

Wrapping my arms tightly around myself, I tiptoed back to my room. I didn't know what unnerved me more: the possibility that Avril was real, or the fact that I could do something and have absolutely no memory of it.

The second time I awoke it was after eight o'clock, and Matt had already left for school. In the bright light the objects in my room—my hairbrush, the romantic paperback, the sweatshirt I'd left draped over a chair—seemed startlingly normal. I got up and began to brush my hair, standing in a swatch of sun-light, hoping it would melt away my uncertainty and fear. Everyone has nightmares, I told myself. As for the change in rooms, I had been sleepwalking.

Arriving downstairs, I found Grandmother pacing. When I greeted her in the hall, she jumped.

"Is everything okay?" I asked.

"My clock is missing."

"Which clock, Grandmother?"

She looked at me as if I should know. "The antique that sat on my desk in the library."

"You mean the little gold one, the one with a pic-ture painted on its face?"

"Where did you put it?" she demanded as if I'd just admitted guilt.

Indignation flared up in me. But I had moved myself without realizing it; how could I be sure I hadn't moved a clock? And the fragment of my dream, a circle with marks on it—wasn't that like the face of a clock?

"I don't remember putting it anywhere," I told her honestly. "Have you asked Matt?"

"No, of course not. I can't trust him anymore."

"Why not?" I asked, walking over to the library door, scanning the shelves and tabletops.

"He has other loyalties now." She said the words slowly, as if they held great meaning.

I moved across the hall to the dining room, my eyes sweeping that room—side tables, windowsills, mantel—any ledge that could support a small clock.

"Grandmother, it's obvious that he loves you and

wants to help you however he can. Though I don't know why, when you're so mean to him."

I walked down the hall and looked in the front parlor. "You were awful last night," I went on. "Matt has a learning disability. It has nothing to do with intelligence, but it makes school hard. You had no right to embarrass him the way you did."

Grandmother raised her head, like a cat picking up a new scent. "Well, now, instead of going after Matt with that smart little mouth of yours, you're defending him."

"I can do both."

"Have you become friends? I believe you have," she said before I could answer. "You're working together, aren't you? He's siding with you now."

I shook my head in amazement and passed her in the hall, crossing over to the music room.

"You two are playing tricks on me!"

"No, Grandmother, we are not."

"Where is the clock?" she asked.

My eyes surveyed the room one more time. "I have no idea."

Fortunately, I had agreed to work for Ginny from ten to three that day and could get away from the house for a while. I didn't mention to her the strange things that had been happening, afraid that she might call my mother or insist I stay with her. I was spooked, but determined to figure out what was going on, which meant I had to stay at the house.

Before I knew it, it was three-fifteen and Ginny was shooing me out the door of Yesterdaze. I walked up High Street and had just passed Tea Leaves, when I heard a girl's voice calling to me.

"Megan. Hey, Megan. Up here!" From a second-story window in the next building, Sophie's ponytail dangled like a fiery flag. "I want to ask you something. Can you come up?"

"Sure," I replied. "Is this where you live?"

Sophie laughed and I stepped back to look at the brick building. It was long, with a porch roof running from end to end, extending over the sidewalk. Next to the front door was a brass lantern and sign: The Mallard Tavern, 1733.

"It's a B and B, bed and breakfast," Sophie explained. "Mom cleans it and I help out after school. Door's open."

I entered the front hall and climbed the carpeted steps, following the sound of a vacuum cleaner. When I arrived on the second floor, the machine shut off and Sophie stuck her head out a door. "The weekenders are gone," she said. "Mom's down washing sheets and towels. Come on in."

The room she was cleaning was homey, with red and white wallpaper, a canopy bed, and chairs pulled close to a small fireplace.

"I looked for you at the dance Saturday night," Sophie said.

I figured she had invited me up to ask about my cousin. "I'd like to have gone, but Matt doesn't want me hanging around his friends. Like I said before, there's really not much I can tell you about him."

"Her," Sophie corrected me.

"Excuse me?"

"It's a *her* I want to ask about." She shook out a clean bottom sheet. "Avril Scarborough. Do you know her?" She watched my face and waited for my response.

"You mean the ghost?"

"Have you seen her?" she asked.

I walked to the other side of the double bed, caught the edge of the sheet, and slipped it over two corners of the mattress. "Have you?"

"I asked you first," she said, then laughed. "Once I did."

"When? Where?"

"Back in sixth grade," she replied, tugging down her corners and smoothing the sheet. "I was still hanging out with Kristy then and she had a sleepover. We paid her older sister to drive us to Scarborough House at four in the morning. Avril usually shows up just before dawn in the back wing."

My breath caught. Then I reminded myself that people would expect to see a ghost in an abandoned part of a house, and people saw what they expected. I had seen what I expected after hearing Alice's story.

"It was a bust," Sophie continued. "Everybody got tired and whiney. Kristy's sister got mad, piled us back in the car, and headed toward town again."

"So when did you see her?"

"That same night, when we were crossing the bridge over Wist Creek."

Sophie shook out a top sheet. We worked together to slip it under the lower end of the mattress and pull it up evenly.

"How do you know what you saw?" I asked. "How do you know it was Avril, or even a she?"

Sophie tossed me a pillow, then thought for a moment. "I guess there was something about the shape. It was thin and moved in a graceful kind of way. She seemed more like a girl than a woman."

"Did anybody else see her that night?"

"Nobody. I got teased a lot," Sophie added, then shrugged. "I've always seen things other people don't, now I just don't tell anyone." We pulled the spread up over the pillows. "I guess you know how that is."

"What do you mean?"

"You're psychic, aren't you?" she asked.

"Me? No!"

Sophie's wide blue eyes studied me. "I was sure you were. I felt a connection."

I frowned and saw the color deepen in her cheeks. She picked up her tray of cleaning supplies and reached for the vacuum. "I've got another room to do."

I followed her across the hall to a room that had different wallpaper but a similar arrangement of bed and furniture. Sophie snatched up a feather duster and began whisking it over frames and mirrors. She didn't look at me.

"I would never have said anything," she explained,

talking a little too fast, "except I thought you were like me. That's why I hoped you had seen the ghost. Psychics seem to attract other forms of spiritual energy—they're like magnets to ghosts. And—well, that's all," she said.

I caught her peeking at me.

"Are you sure you're not?" she asked. "You've never been aware of things that other people aren't? You've never had an experience you can't explain?"

"No," I lied.

She shook her head. "I read you wrong."

"Except," I said, "some, uh, strange dreams."

"Miss Lydia says that dreams are shadows cast by truth shining on our darkest secrets."

"Well, mine aren't all that mysterious," I replied. "I can explain them—most of them."

I told Sophie about my childhood visits to a house that looked like Grandmother's and my recent dream of the dollhouse, along with my theories about seeing photos of Mom with the miniature house.

"You could be right," Sophie said, sounding unconvinced.

"You have a better explanation?"

"You're psychic—telepathic. When you were little, your mom was watching you play and thinking about herself as a kid at home. You picked up the images and made them your own."

"I like my theory better."

"Okay by me," Sophie said agreeably. She lifted a sheet from a pile on a chair, and we went to work making the bed.

"Who's Miss Lydia?" I asked.

"The old lady who owns the café next door. Jamie Riley's mother."

"Oh!"

"When I was little," Sophie went on, "and Mom was working here at the Mallard, I'd go to Tea Leaves for my after-school snack. Miss Lydia liked me and talked to me a lot."

"She sure doesn't like me," I said, then told Sophie about my introduction to the woman.

"Don't be offended," Sophie advised. "Miss Lydia doesn't trust many people. A couple years ago she got in trouble for selling her herbal remedies at the Queen Victoria, the hotel across the street. Guests complained. A woman said she got sick, but that can happen with herbal stuff, just like it does with a prescription from a doctor. Anyway, now Miss Lydia only deals with locals and keeps thinking guys from the FBI are coming after her."

"If she's psychic, wouldn't she know they aren't?"

Sophie didn't laugh and didn't get annoyed. "No. Just because you're psychic doesn't mean you can see clearly. Sometimes the more you see, the more confusing it is. Images overlap and it's hard to sort them out."

We finished making the bed in silence. Sophie kept her head down as if she were deep in thought. When she looked up, her eyes were bright. "How about an O.B.E.? Out-of-body experience? Some people do that, you know. Their spirit breaks free of their body and travels around. Maybe you were curious about your grandmother and came to see her as a child."

"Without my body?" I said, looking at Sophie like she was crazy.

"Well, yes and no," she replied. "Your body would be back where you left it. But if your grandmother were psychically aware, she'd have seen an apparition of you that looked like your body."

I kept quiet.

"I'm making you uncomfortable," Sophie observed. She stuck the vacuum cleaner plug in a wall socket. "This is all I have left to do. Thanks for stopping by." She waited for me to leave, her finger on the trigger of the machine.

"Have you seen *Sheer Blue?*" I asked.

"The movie?" she replied. "No."

"Want to go?"

She looked surprised, then smiled. "Didn't scare you away, huh?"

"Not yet."

"How about Thursday night?" she suggested. "We're off school Friday."

"Great."

The vacuum roared to life and I left. As I walked up High Street, I wondered to myself what secrets were casting shadows long enough to reach into my dreams.

nine

When I arrived home that afternoon, I found my grandmother sitting in the kitchen, idly watching her housekeeper fix dinner. Grandmother's skin was so pale it seemed translucent, her hands clasped but in constant motion, as if she couldn't keep them warm.

"Are you okay?" I asked, quickly setting down my purse. "Has something happened, Grandmother?"

She didn't reply.

I glanced over at Nancy. "What's wrong?"

"Don't know. She won't say," Nancy replied, then shoved a runny casserole into the oven. "I've tried all afternoon to get her to see the doctor. No use wasting your breath—she won't go. She's been spooky ever since I found that little clock."

"You found the clock?" I asked, my mouth dry.

"Now, don't *you* get funny on me."

"Where was it?"

"On the hall table, behind the silk flowers."

I pulled a chair up close to Grandmother and sat down. "How are you feeling?"

"Fine."

"You don't look it. I want to call your doctor."

"I forbid you," she said.

Nancy gave me an I-told-you-so look.

"As you know, Grandmother, I don't always listen."

"You may call, but I won't go."

I stood up. "Matt should be home soon. He'll know what to do."

Nancy shook her head. "He called and Mrs. Barnes told him he could stay at Alex's." The woman sounded exasperated. "She could have told me earlier. All the time I put into that casserole, and her with no appetite and you a vegetarian."

"I eat meat," I said.

"Take it out when the buzzer goes off," Nancy went on. "You can dig around for the peas."

I didn't correct her a second time, just waited for her to leave, hoping Grandmother would talk to me then. But as soon as Nancy was gone, Grandmother retreated to her room. I followed her upstairs and told her I would check on her in an hour.

"You will not," she said, then closed the door. I heard the lock click.

I ate alone in the kitchen that evening, glad to be away from the gory deer in the dining room. Afterward, I went to the library to see the antique clock. I weighed it in my hands and ran my fingers over its cold metal surfaces, hoping they would remember what my mind did not: Was this the first time I'd held it? Could I have moved it before I went to the rose-papered room? I set the clock down gently, knowing no more than I did before.

At ten o'clock Matt still hadn't come back from Alex's. I found the number and called to tell Matt the situation. He said he'd check on Grandmother when he got home. I went to bed, leaving my bedroom door cracked, knowing I wouldn't sleep.

Twenty minutes later Matt knocked softly on Grandmother's door, calling to her. The door creaked open. I slipped out of bed and went to the entrance of my room. Though I couldn't make out Matt's words, I knew from his tone he was asking questions.

Grandmother was upset and either forgot I was in the next room or didn't care. She spoke loudly. "I have brought it on myself, Matt."

He quietly asked her something else.

"I have brought it on myself!" she repeated, sounding frustrated. "Don't you understand? I'm being punished."

"But there's nothing for you to be punished for," Matt replied, his voice growing as intense as hers.

"God has chosen her as his instrument," Grandmother insisted.

"God hasn't chosen anything," he argued. "You were the one who invited Megan. Things are being misplaced, Grandmother, nothing more. It's all in your head."

Her response was muffled with emotion.

"Hush! Everything's going to be all right," he said. Then I heard him take a step inside the room. The door closed.

Cut off from their conversation, I closed my own door and rested back against it. Their conference lasted a long time. Finally I heard Grandmother's door open and close again, then Matt's footsteps in the hall, heading in the direction of the stairway. He stopped at my door. I knew he was standing on the other side and I waited for him to knock.

When I heard him walk away, I quickly opened the door. He turned around.

"Is she going to be okay?" I asked.

His mouth formed a grim line. "She's confused. If she doesn't get better, I'm taking her to a doctor."

"And you?" I saw how shaken he looked. "How are *you* doing?"

"You don't have to worry about me."

"Do anyway."

He looked away.

I stepped into the hall. "Matt, why is she acting this way?"

"You should never have come here, Megan."

"Are you saying it's my fault?" I asked. "Are you? Please look at me."

He did, and for a moment neither of us spoke.

"Are you asking me to leave?"

He took a deep breath. "It would be the best thing."

"Okay, I'll consider it, but first tell me why she's upset. I want to know what's going on."

He didn't reply.

"Matt, I can't help if I don't understand the problem."

Still he said nothing.

"So I guess you don't want my help."

"I don't."

I stepped back into my room and closed the door. The distance he kept between us no longer made me mad; it made me hurt.

We were playing a game, Matt and I. I was tiptoeing around an abandoned house—or maybe it was a barn. The walls and floors were made of rough wood, and the simple wooden stairs looked more like tilted ladders. We were playing hide-and-seek.

It was twilight outside. Inside, it grew darker with each minute. I knew we should stop the game before it got too late, but I kept on. I could hear Matt walking on the floor above my head, searching for me. I quietly opened a trapdoor and descended the stairs that led to the basement.

The air was cold and damp down there; it held the darkness like a sponge. My eyes adjusted slowly to the bit of light that came from the doorway above. Suddenly I saw huge wheels, wheels with teeth, one wheel interlocking with the next, like the gears inside a clock. The largest was as tall as I.

I heard a noise, a groan from the machinery. My

eyes focused on the biggest wheel. It started to turn slowly, very slowly at first. The smaller wheels rotated with it. I had to stop them. I knew if I didn't, they'd turn faster and faster, shaking the old building till it flew apart.

I grasped the huge teeth of the main wheel and pulled back, dragging it in the opposite direction. But as soon as I stopped pulling, the wheel moved forward again, turning more quickly. I gripped harder, my hands slippery with sweat. Still, each time I pulled back, the gigantic wheel made up those inches and moved even farther ahead, pulling me with it.

I had to find another way to stop it. I tried to step back to study the wheel and discovered I couldn't move. I yanked my arm, struggling to pull it away, but the edge of my sweater sleeve was caught between the teeth of the big wheel and a smaller one. The speed of the wheels was steadily increasing. I called for help, called for Matt. I writhed and pulled and bit the threads of my sweater. At the last moment I slipped free of it.

Run, I told myself. But I stood there, fascinated, watching the wheels consume my garment. Then I felt the pull. The powerful teeth had caught my hair. I was being dragged toward the center of the wheels. I screamed for Matt.

I heard his footsteps cross the floor above me. I shouted his name over and over. Then I heard his footsteps fading and the door upstairs shut. He had left me.

I struggled to free myself, fighting for each inch against the powerful wheels, dreading the teeth that would crush whatever came between them.

I couldn't believe Matt had abandoned me. Then I thought, he knows what's happening. He started these wheels moving. That instant I was pulled into the darkness.

ten

In the morning light last night's dream had lost its terror but not its power to disturb. I recognized the exaggerations of a nightmare—huge wheels, like gears inside a gigantic clock, waiting to grind me up—it was surreal. Even so, I felt a sense of foreboding. What truth lay behind the images? In the dream I had been drawn into something I had no control over, something I couldn't stop, and Matt had walked away.

I dressed slowly, then went down to the kitchen. Matt was there, finishing a bowl of cereal.

"How's Grandmother?" I asked. "*Where's* Grandmother?"

Her Bible lay open on the table next to a half-drained cup of coffee.

"In the music room," he said wearily.

"Why?"

"Don't you know?" he snapped.

I bit back a sharp response. "Something else has been moved."

"How did you know it was moved, rather than missing?" he asked, as if trying to trap me in my words.

"Ease up, Matt. When we thought the Bible and clock were missing, it turned out they were moved."

He rubbed his head. He looked as if he'd barely slept.

"So what was it this time?"

"Paintings. An old painting of the mill was moved from the parlor to the music room and hung above the Chinese chest. The watercolor that was there was left facedown on the floor."

"When did this happen?"

"You tell me. You were here last night, alone in the house while she was up in bed."

"Are you accusing me?" I asked.

"I don't know what I'm doing," he mumbled.

I intercepted him as he walked toward the refrigerator. "You have as much access to this house as I do, and know the place better. We can point fingers at each other and refuse to trust or we can try—"

The kitchen door opened.

Grandmother gazed at the two of us, her eyes narrowing. Matt and I stepped back from each other.

"I have put the watercolor where it belongs," she informed us. "I need help with the landscape."

"I'll take care of it," I said. "You'll be late for school,

Matt. Leave me the phone number of Grandmother's doctor," I added, when she had exited.

I followed her through the door and down the hall to the front parlor, where I helped her set the large painting back on its hook.

"Is there anything else I can do?" I asked.

"Haven't you done enough?" Grandmother replied sarcastically.

I stared after her as she left the room. If I didn't get some answers soon, I was going to be as paranoid as she. I needed information, and there was only one person I knew who might have it.

I arrived at Tea Leaves an hour before work.

"I don't want my fortune read," I said to Jamie. "Tell your mother I have some questions about my grandmother's house and the family. Strange things are happening, and I need her advice."

A few minutes later the door opened at the top of the stairs, and the old woman beckoned to me. Before I reached the entrance to the second-floor apartment, Mrs. Riley had disappeared around the corner. I closed the door behind me and followed her down a narrow hall that ran toward the front of the building.

The room I entered had three windows, all of them facing High Street. Heavy drapes hung lopsided from their rods but were open enough to let in light. To the left were two sofas with faded print covers, and to the right an alcove, a square area between the front wall of the building and the wall of the stairwell. A round table and several straight-back chairs filled that space. A silk lamp with fringe hung from the ceiling.

Mrs. Riley sat down at the table, facing into the room, and gestured to a seat across from her. I perched on it nervously, tucking my hands under my legs.

"You have questions," she said.

I nodded. "I'm not sure where to begin."

"Strange things have been happening at the house." Her voice was low, almost soothing. "What kind of things?"

"Well, objects are being moved. The Bible, for instance. It was missing from its shelf in the kitchen, and Grandmother became convinced that someone had stolen it. Later, I spotted it in the library. Instead of being glad I found it, she was angry and kept staring at the spot it had occupied."

"Which was on a library shelf," Mrs. Riley said.

"Yes, just to the left of the fireplace."

The psychic's head lifted slightly. "Tell me more."

Feeling a little more comfortable, I rested my hands on the table. "This morning we found that a picture had been moved from the front parlor to the music room. Grandmother started getting weird again—paranoid, as if someone were doing this to her, as if *I* were doing it.

"A painting," she repeated.

"A landscape," I said. "A picture of a mill."

Mrs. Riley didn't make a sound, but I saw the buttons on her dress move and catch the light as if she had quickly sucked in a breath.

"Yesterday a clock was missing from Grand-mother's desk."

"A small clock . . . an old one," she murmured.

"Yes. It has a picture painted on its face, roses and—"

"Was it found on the hall table?"

I blinked. "How did you know?"

She sat back in her chair. "That is where it used to be kept. The Bible always sat on a shelf by the library's hearth. The mill painting hung over the Chinese chest in the music room."

"You mean things are being moved back to where they were years ago? To where they were when you worked there?"

She nodded her head slowly, rhythmically.

"But then why would Grandmother blame me? How would I know where those things were kept? I don't see how Matt would know, either, unless Grandmother told him."

Mrs. Riley's eyes closed, then drifted open again. She looked past me as if she were looking into another world. She stared for so long I turned around to see what was there. Nothing extraordinary—a flow-ered sofa, a table piled with Baggies, her herbal stuff.

"The clock belonged to Avril," Mrs. Riley said. "She insisted on placing it in the hall. She hated the big grandfather clock."

"I don't blame her," I remarked. "It's like a guard stationed on the landing, watching you come in and out. You can hear it tolling wherever you are in the house."

"Avril called it the big bully. She would reset the small clock to whatever time she wanted it to be. Her parents played along, allowing her to come home long after she was supposed to. I'm surprised your grandmother didn't throw out that wretched little clock."

"It's an antique."

"What's one more antique?" Mrs. Riley said. "Helen has money to burn."

"Maybe she keeps it because it reminds her of Avril."

"That's precisely why she would throw it out."

I was surprised by the bitterness in Mrs. Riley's voice. "Did you work there when Avril was alive?" I asked.

"I was the personal maid of both girls."

"But you must have been their age."

"A year older than Avril," she replied, "two years older than Helen."

That couldn't have been easy, I thought, especially if Avril acted like a princess. "What were they like, my grandmother and Avril?"

Mrs. Riley took a deep breath and let it out slowly. "Avril was pretty, popular, and spoiled. She was always into something and got too much attention from her parents. Poor, serious Helen got almost nothing."

"That doesn't sound fair."

"Helen was a good girl. She read a lot and always kept her room neat. It was nothing for me to pick up after her. But Avril! She didn't care where she threw things, and her room was small and crowded. She insisted on sleeping in the back wing."

"The back wing?" I sat up a little straighter.

"Oh, I knew what she was up to, even if her parents didn't. She could get in and out of the house by way of the kitchen roof."

I put my hand over my mouth. Avril had slept in the room where I'd awakened, where Alice had seen the ghost.

"What is it?" Mrs. Riley asked.

"Nothing."

The pupils of her eyes were like dark pins tacking me to the wall; she wouldn't let me go until I gave a better answer.

"I've been in that room," I said at last. "It has roses on the wallpaper."

"Avril adored roses. She wanted them in vases, in her hair, in bouquets brought by her boyfriends, and she always got what she wanted. Poor Helen grew terribly jealous and angry. I didn't blame her, not after Avril stole Thomas."

"But my grandfather was Thomas," I said, puzzled.

Mrs. Riley nodded, her eyes long, dark slits, as if focusing on a distant memory. "He was Helen's beau first—at least publicly. There were other girls, many others. *Money* is what made up Thomas's mind."

It wasn't a flattering picture of my mother's father, but I had come for the truth.

"He was a young cabinetmaker from Philadelphia,

an apprentice hired to do repair work at Scarborough House," Mrs. Riley continued. "Thomas was talented but had no money. He switched his affections from Helen to Avril, who, as the oldest, was supposed to inherit Scarborough House. When Avril died, everything became Helen's. Everything including Thomas."

I sat back in my chair thinking about how Grandmother must have felt, dumped, then picked up again, second choice. Still, it happened so long ago. "I don't understand why any of this would matter to her now, but something has set her off, and it seems connected to Avril."

"Some wounds heal, others fester," Mrs. Riley replied.

"Have you seen the ghost at Scarborough House?" I asked.

"No. Not long after Avril died, I married and left the house. I have never been invited back."

"Is it possible that my grandmother thinks she is being haunted by the ghost of her dead sister?"

Mrs. Riley ran her gnarled hands over the table, touching it with just the tips of her fingers, as if she were using a Ouija board.

"Why do you say *thinks?*" she asked. "Because you don't believe it's possible?"

"I don't know. I really don't. Can a ghost move things?"

"Yes," she replied.

"Can a ghost"—I hesitated—"lead a person somewhere, guide a person to a room or place?"

"Certainly you have heard accounts of ghosts revealing where they've hidden valuables," she said.

"How did Avril die?"

Mrs. Riley studied me long and hard. "Do you want the real story, or the one the family told?"

"Both."

"According to the family doctor, according to what Mr. and Mrs. Scarborough wanted him to say, it was an allergic reaction."

"To what?"

"Redcreep. It grows here on the Shore. Since colonial times, girls and women have used mixtures of it as a beauty potion. It dilates the eyes, brings color into the cheeks. They found a bottle on Avril's bureau."

"And the real story?" I asked.

"It was an overdose. Avril, like a lot of girls back then, had taken redcreep before. She wasn't allergic to it. She was sneaking out to see Thomas that night—Helen and I both knew it—and wanted to look pretty. She became ill at the mill, which was their secret meeting place. Thomas rushed her to the doctor, but she died on the way. An overdose of redcreep. Even good things can harm you if too much is taken at one time. So typical of Avril," she added, "always wanting to do more, try more, have more, always flaunting limits.

"The family did not want a cause like 'overdose' to be listed in the paper. That would make Avril responsible, and she never got blamed for anything. Of course, the Scarboroughs had their way, as money always does."

Mrs. Riley rested her chin on her hands. Her voice sounded tired, as if the bitter edge I'd heard earlier had turned, and all she could feel now was the flat of the knife.

"I guess that's most of my questions," I said. "How much should I pay you?"

"There is no charge for today," she replied, rising with me.

"Really, I planned to," I told her, but she refused the money and led the way to the door.

"I would send your grandmother my regards," she said, opening the door to downstairs, "but I doubt that would please her. It would be best not to mention that you saw me today."

"Why?"

"It's free advice, girl," she replied. "Take it or leave it."

"Thanks," I said, and took a step down, which was a good thing since she closed the door on my heel.

eleven

I grabbed breakfast downstairs at the café then headed for work at Yesterdaze. Ginny was incredibly patient with me that day. I had to count a pack of singles four times before I got it right and gave her nickels when she asked for dimes. At 3:10 I apologized for my mistakes.

She smiled. "Don't worry about it. Are we still on for Wednesday, Thursday, and Saturday?"

"Yup."

Ginny was giving me Friday off to rest up for "the weekend invasion."

Instead of going home after work, I wandered up and down High Street and the streets around it, thinking about the things I'd learned from Mrs. Riley. I didn't see the Jeep pass by, not until Alex hung out the back, waving and calling my name. It stopped a half block ahead of me and two girls got out, Kristy and one of her echoes. They looked in my direction, then quickly turned away and said something to the guys.

As soon as they started up the walk, Alex called out, "Hey, Megan, where you going?"

"Nowhere special," I answered as I got closer. "Just walking."

"Want a ride?" he asked.

I glanced at Matt, hoping for an invitation from him. He said nothing.

"Climb in," Alex encouraged me. "You can ride up front."

"I don't know if I want a ride that bad," I told him. "I saw how Matt drove the first day I was in town."

"How did I drive?" Matt asked.

"You nearly took Ginny's fender with you."

He frowned. "You sure? I didn't see you."

"No kidding!"

Alex laughed, then Matt smiled and reached across the seat to open the door. I climbed in.

We drove to a street of Victorian homes that faced the college campus, stopping in front of a tall white house with green shutters and a wraparound porch. Alex hopped out on the passenger side, then leaned on the edge of my door.

"Would you go out with me?" he asked.

I didn't expect the question. "Um . . ." I started to turn toward Matt.

Alex reached up and caught my face lightly with his hand. "You don't need his permission, do you?"

"I guess not." I heard my cousin's seat squeak. "It's just that I'm not here for very long, and I don't want to screw up the friendship you guys have."

"If Matt doesn't like me going out with you, then *he's* screwing up the friendship, right?"

I thought about it, then smiled. "Right. So when?"

"Thursday night? We don't have school Friday and there's a big party at Kristy's."

"Oh, no, sorry. Sophie and I are going to a movie."

He looked surprised. "Can't you change it? I thought girls had a rule that when one of them got asked for a date, all other plans were off."

"I don't go by that rule."

Behind me Matt laughed, a little too loudly, I thought.

"It's not fair to the other person," I explained. "Especially Sophie. She's got enough to do with school and work. I don't want to change plans on her."

"You mean Sophie Quinn?" Alex asked. "We used to be best buddies when we were in grade school. Why don't the four of us go to the party—you, me, Sophie, and Matt?"

Now I did turn to my cousin.

He shrugged. "Okay with me."

"I'll ask Sophie what she wants to do," I told Alex, though I was pretty sure she'd be thrilled to be Matt's date.

Alex probably thought the same thing, for he gave the door a satisfied thump. "See you Thursday night."

As we pulled away from the curb, I said to Matt, "Don't worry about me and your friends. I'll be on my good behavior."

"I was just getting used to you," he replied, "and now you're going to change?"

"I can't win with you!" I exclaimed.

"Didn't know you wanted to."

I shook my head and sighed. "Listen, Matt, before we get to the house, we have to talk."

"About Grandmother," he guessed, and slowed down a little. "Did she get worse after I left?"

"Not worse, but she's really starting to get to me, the way she blames me for the things that are moved. I needed some information so I could figure out what was going on. I went to see Mrs. Riley."

The firm set of his mouth and long silence told me he didn't like what I had done.

"She used to work for the Scarboroughs," I went on, "back when Grandmother and Aunt Avril were teens. Did you know that?"

"I knew she had worked at the house." He flicked the Jeep's blinker with one finger, then made a sharp turn. "And I know better than to trust her."

"She told me that the Bible, the clock, and the painting were moved back to where they used to be years ago, when Avril was alive."

He glanced sideways at me. I couldn't see enough of his face to know if he was surprised by the news.

"Mrs. Riley has a way of coaxing information out of people," he said, "then feeding it back to them in a different form, so that they think she's telling them something new."

"But she guessed where the clock was found. And though I told her the landscape was moved to the music room, she knew it was hung over the Chinese chest."

"Megan, think about the size of the painting. Where else would you hang it in the music room? As for the clock, a lot of people keep them in entrance halls. Every old house in Maryland has a grandfather clock in the hall or on the stairway landing."

"It's too much of a coincidence," I insisted.

"Mrs. Riley makes her living off coincidences. I hope you didn't pay her a lot."

"She didn't charge," I replied somewhat smugly.

"She's counting on you to come back. Then she'll charge double," he said, sounding just as smug.

We rumbled across the Wist bridge. I turned back to look at it, remembering that Sophie had seen the ghost there. Didn't ghosts haunt battlefields and other places where they died? If Avril had died somewhere between the mill and the doctor's, could it have been while Thomas was driving over the bridge?

"Where's the mill?" I asked.

"On the creek. About a third of a mile beyond Grandmother's driveway there's a road to the left. It runs down to the mill."

"We've got some time," I said. "Let's go."

"No," he responded quickly.

"Why not?"

"There's nothing to see," he said. "It's been abandoned for years and is full of mice and rats."

"Okay, I'll go later without you."

He shook his head. "Pigheaded."

"Yeah," I agreed, "amazing, isn't it? We're not related by blood, but we share that family trait."

"Listen to me, Megan, you can't go inside the mill. Most of it's made of wood, and it's rotting. The structure's unsafe."

As he said that, he drove past Grandmother's driveway. I tried not to smile.

"Don't smirk," he told me.

"Another family trait."

"I'm taking you there so you don't go by yourself," he said. "Understand?"

"Yes. Thank you, big brother."

Mutual smirk.

The road down to the mill was bumpy, its stone and shell layer worn away, leaving long bare spots and deep ruts. Bushes and small trees grew close to the road and scratched the sides of the Jeep. Matt muttered a few choice words. Then suddenly we were in a clearing with a sea of tall grass washing around us. The soft weathered wood of the mill rose above it, two stories, topped by an attic under a sloping roof.

"It's the one in the painting," I said.

Matt nodded.

A structure like a dormer window projected out of the middle of the steep roof, but it was larger, framing a door. The roof door gaped open, leaving a dark cavity in the light gray building. The first and second stories had doors that lined up beneath the roof entrance, but they were closed, as was a side door. All the windows were shuttered.

"Where's the waterwheel?" I asked.

"Around the side."

I got out of the Jeep.

"Megan? Don't go inside."

"I'll be back."

A moment later he trudged behind me to the bank of a stream that ran toward the basement wall of the mill. The large, motionless wheel next to the wall looked like the rusty paddle wheel of a steamboat.

"Not exactly rushing water," I observed.

"The mill works from a pond," Matt explained, pointing toward a rise in ground on the other side of the road. "When the gates are opened, the water comes in over the top of the wheel, using gravity to turn it."

I nodded, then gazed up again at the dark entrance into the roof. "Have you ever seen a ghost here?"

"There is no ghost," he replied.

"This is where Avril came, the day she died."

He looked at me surprised. "How do you know that?"

"Mrs. Riley told me. She said Avril came with our grandfather. Thomas was Grandmother's boyfriend first, then Avril stole him from her. This was Thomas and Avril's secret meeting place."

"I don't believe it."

"Do you have any reason not to?" I asked.

"Mrs. Riley is a gossip and she's always been out to get our family."

"That's a pretty flimsy reason."

"We've spent enough time here," he told me abruptly, then started toward the Jeep.

I caught up with him. "Mrs. Riley said–"

"I think it'd be a good idea," he interrupted, "if you, Lydia Riley, and Grandmother started living in the present."

"Not knowing what happened in the past can keep you from living fully in the present."

"It's not relevant," he argued, and opened the door on my side of the Jeep. "Get in."

"No."

He reached for my arm.

I pulled back, but he held on, so tightly I winced. "You're hurting me!"

He let go.

"I have some more looking to do."

Matt leaned against the Jeep and said nothing.

I headed around the other side of the mill. As the land sloped down to the water the ground beneath my feet became soft and claylike, perhaps flooded by the creek, which was about twenty feet away. The mill looked tall from the creek side, four stories of it towering above me, the basement's brick wall exposed. At the base of the building was a Dutch door, its lower half open. It was an inviting mouse hole–and people hole.

I walked over to the double door and pushed on the top half. It didn't budge. I knelt and crawled through the bottom, tumbling into the darkness head-first—there were two steps down on the inside. The floor was wet, covered with gross stuff. Ahead of me I could see nothing but vague shapes. Standing up, I turned toward the door and ran my hands over the top portion until I felt a bolt. After several tries, I slid it back and pulled open the upper half of the door, letting in more light.

When I turned to face the basement again, I gasped. At the far end of the long room were wheels—big gears—one interlocking with the next, the largest as tall as I. I was in the basement of my dream, where I had hidden from Matt. I sank down on the doorstep, afraid to cross to the other side, afraid to get close to those wheels.

How had I come to dream of this place? I doubted I was reading the images of my *mother's* mind. The voice, the dreams, awakening in Avril's room, the movement of objects to where Avril would expect them—it was Avril I was connecting with.

My skin felt cold and clammy. I stood up quickly. "Leave me alone," I said, stumbling out of the entrance. "Just leave me alone!"

Matt, who had been hovering a short distance away, heard me. He stepped back, turned abruptly, and strode up the hill to his Jeep.

*   *   *

Neither of us spoke on the way home. I knew Matt thought that I was telling him to leave me alone, but there wasn't much I could do about it. He wouldn't believe I had been talking to a ghost.

He parked in front of the house and got out of the Jeep without glancing at me. Following him up the porch steps, I noticed the clay and mud caked on the thick rubber soles of his Nikes.

"Our shoes are a mess," I said, sitting down on a bench to remove mine. He checked his, then sat opposite me. By the time he started unlacing his shoes, mine were off and I was carrying them into the house.

Grandmother met me, coming through the door from the back wing. "You're late."

"For dinner?" I glanced up at the landing clock. It wasn't five yet.

She stared at my shoes. "What were you doing after work?"

"Hanging out."

Matt came in the door and Grandmother's eyes darted to his shoes. Color rose in her cheeks. "Where have you been?"

Though the question was fired at him, I answered, since the trip had been my idea. "To the mill."

"Why did you take her there?" Grandmother demanded, still focusing on Matt.

I saw the wary look on his face. "I asked him to," I said.

"I'm not talking to *you*."

"Megan wanted to see the place," Matt replied, "and I thought it'd be safer if I went with her."

"Megan wanted to see the place," Grandmother mimicked.

"I did," I said. "I was curious."

Grandmother took a step toward me. "I told you the day you came that I expected you to respect my privacy. Didn't I?"

I nodded silently.

"I'm speaking to you now. Answer me aloud!"

"Yes, Grandmother." I couldn't snap at her. If I was feeling haunted by Avril's presence, I could only imagine how she felt.

"So now you're going to be sweet and soft-spoken," she observed, her lips curling. "Sweet and sneaky."

"Ease up, Grandmother," Matt said. "Did you ever tell Megan not to go to the mill?"

"Are you defending her?"

"All I'm saying is you're getting all worked up over a little visit to the mill," he replied.

"And Lydia Riley," she added.

I looked at Grandmother, surprised. "Who told you that?"

"It doesn't matter. What matters is that you promise not to speak to her again."

"Why?"

"Don't talk back to me!" Her voice was shrill.

I sat down on the steps, hoping to make this a conversation rather than an irrational shouting match.

"I wasn't talking back," I explained. "I was just wondering—"

"You're living in my house, you'll follow my rules."

I bit my lip, then nodded.

Matt rested a hand on her arm. "Grandmother, be fair. Megan was just asking—"

She turned on him. "I don't have to explain my rules to anyone, including you, Matt." Her jaw began to shake. "I can't trust you anymore. Not since *she's* come."

"What do you mean?" he asked.

"You're loyal to her now."

He stared at Grandmother. It was as if he had to be on her side, or my side, and wasn't allowed to care about both of us at the same time.

"Get a hold of yourself," he said, and walked out the back door of the hall.

Grandmother stood in front of me, her head held high, then strode into the library and shut the door behind her.

I remained sitting on the steps, bewildered by her jealous suspicions. Some wounds heal, others fester, Mrs. Riley had said. Maybe Grandmother had never really healed from her first betrayal. Matt was the most significant person in her life now, and she the most consistent person in his. I wondered if she saw me as someone like Avril, putting myself between them. Maybe Grandmother was afraid of losing out again.

Well, that was her problem. She was the one who

chose to spin her world around one grandchild, reject-
ing my parents and brothers and me. I rose and
climbed the stairs, feeling torn between pity and
anger. Then I heard the machinery of the big clock
begin to wind. I took the steps two at a time, hurrying
past before it could start its dismal tolling.

twelve

Wednesday morning I saw Matt just long enough to ask if I could pick up my e-mail from his computer. When he'd left for school, Grandmother informed me that she had an early appointment. I didn't ask where, not after yesterday's reminder about her privacy. She drove off and I went upstairs to retrieve my mail. I had several messages from friends at home, but it was Mom's letter I was most eager to open. I printed it out, deleted the electronic copy, then sat back to read.

Hi, Sweetheart!
Dad and I loved your e-mail. We felt like we were back on High Street again.
Life here isn't the same without you. Pete and Dave have both said they miss you, though I

promised them I wouldn't squeal (crossed my fingers).

In your note you barely mentioned Grandmother. I know you, Megan, and I worry when you get silent. I'm counting on you to let me know if there's a problem.

So you found the dollhouse! It was built for Grandmother and her sister. I played with it as a kid, but I can't find a photo of it anywhere. Why do you ask?

About Aunt Avril. Neither Mother nor Dad spoke much of her. I've never even seen her picture—perhaps they were all put away when she died. We weren't supposed to ask questions about her. Dad said it made Mother sad to think about her sister. I do remember putting birthday flowers on her grave in April—Avril is the French word for that month. In October, too—I think that's when she died. She had a close friend named Angel, Angel Cayton. Angel's father was a doctor, and someone told me that Avril was brought to him the night she died. That's as much as I know.

Everyone's well here. The Naughtons' spaniel had puppies. Write soon. And this time don't leave out whatever you were trying to skirt around in your last e-mail.

Love,
Mom

I printed out my friends' notes, then logged off. As soon as I got to work, I'd ask Ginny to help me find Avril's friend.

"Angel Cayton," Ginny said, stuffing tissue down the arms of a pale silk dress that was decorated with seed pearls. She and I had put the dress on a seamstress form so Ginny could photograph it for an out-of-town client. "I haven't thought about her in ages. She died fifteen, no, must be twenty years ago now. Angel was a character—very active in town affairs and generous with her money. She started the Watermen's Fund."

"Did she leave behind any family?" I asked, though I had little hope of someone remembering stories they were told more than twenty years ago.

"I don't think so. Evie?"

Evie Brown, one of our elderly customers who came by almost every day, was standing in front of a mirror, trying purses on her arm.

"Evie, do you know if Angel Cayton has any family left around here?"

Miss Brown chewed over the name for a moment. "Nope," she said at last. "Angel was an only child and never married. Her sweetheart, Sam Tighe, died in the last war."

"That's World War II," Ginny whispered to me.

"Angel got killed in a car accident, didn't she—yes, I'm sure," Miss Brown answered herself. "Out Talbot Road on Dead Man's Curve. Though Angel was the only one who ever died there. Why we don't call it

Dead Woman's Curve, I just don't know. The county never gets things straight."

"I don't think the county named the curve," Ginny said gently.

"State's just as bad," the woman responded, then reached for a red purse on a peg beyond her grasp. I walked over and lifted it down.

"Sorry we can't help you out," Ginny told me.

"What's the problem?" the old woman asked, taking the red purse from me, then looping the others she had tried on my arm, as if I were a store rack.

"I was hoping to talk to Miss Cayton," I replied.

"Then try Lydia Riley. She's good at ringing through to the other side."

I heard Ginny swallow a giggle.

"I'm surprised your grandmother didn't suggest that," Evie added. "Helen was over there today."

She added the red purse to my arm.

"Over where?"

"Seeing Lydia Riley. Right before my appointment this morning."

"Are you sure?"

"Are you saying I get mixed up?" Miss Brown asked, her eyes flashing.

'No, no. I'm surprised, that's all."

"Me, too," she agreed amiably. "Far as I know, they haven't spoken for years. Can't imagine what they had to talk about." She peered up at me inquisitively. "Can you?"

"No," I said, imagining a *lot* of things.

* * *

Sophie dropped by the shop that afternoon. After finishing up with a customer, I joined her at the jewelry case. She was leaning on her elbows, gazing down at the aquamarine pendant.

"Guess what?" I said. "We have another invite for tomorrow night. A party."

She straightened up and smiled. "Whose? The only party I know about is Kristy's."

"That's it."

Her face fell. "I wasn't invited, and I don't think Kristy would be thrilled if I just showed up. I haven't been part of her crowd since middle school. You go to the party, and we can see the movie Friday night."

"But you're not crashing it," I told her. "Matt is asking you."

"Matt?" Sophie's cheeks grew pink. "Kristy will kill me!"

"But I thought you liked him. And I thought you said he doesn't date one person."

"I do like him. And he doesn't date one person. And she'll still be mad as anything."

"Who cares? You can talk to me at the party. I'm going with Alex."

"Oh! I have to think about this, Megan."

"Alex said you used to be best friends."

"Yeah, forever ago." Sophie went over to the silk dress Ginny had put on the seamstress form and traced its seed pearl design with her finger. Ginny came out of the storeroom, eyed Sophie, then eyed the dress. She held her head to one side and squinted, an action that usually meant we were about to rearrange a display.

Sophie turned back to me. "Alex and I used to spend every day together at school and during the summer, crabbing time," she said. "He could always convince me to chicken neck off the bridge at four in the morning. I was the only person who'd go out with him in his old boat in pouring rain to set a trot line. I really liked being around him and the water."

"Then this should be fun."

Sophie didn't look so sure. "I hope he's forgotten about the valentine I sent him in fifth grade."

"Why?" I asked.

"It was so embarrassing. Alex wanted to hang out with the guys, and they wouldn't let a girl tag along. I wanted him to know he was important to me, so I made him this valentine heart. I drew crab legs around it for lace, and a boat oar for the arrow."

I laughed out loud and Sophie blushed.

"One of his friends found it and showed it to everyone. They teased him awful. That was pretty much it for Alex and his *girl* friend."

She paused and watched Ginny, who opened the jewelry case and took out the aquamarine pendant.

"Listen, Sophie," I said, "if there's one thing I've learned about guys, it's that they don't remember sentimental things, not even a heart with crab legs for lace. Besides, that was fifth grade. I think Alex has changed his mind about hanging out with girls."

She laughed a little. "I guess so."

"So think about it," I told her. "We'll do whatever you want to do."

"Sophie, don't go anywhere," Ginny said. "I need a favor. Would you put on this dress and let me take your picture?"

"The pearl dress? Oh, my gosh!" Sophie gasped.

"I think that's a yes," I said.

Ginny undid the buttons and removed the dress from the form. "Let's see now," she said, talking to herself more than us, "we're going to need some shoes, and let's put your hair up on your head, so a nice comb, soft ivory pearls for that red hair." Ginny picked up an armful of items, then ushered Sophie to the dressing room in the back.

I served two customers, waiting for Sophie to come out. When the bells hanging on the shop door jingled a third time, I looked up to see Alex and Matt in their running clothes.

"Let me guess," I said, "you're interested in lace hankies."

Alex grinned. "Do you have any that match our shorts?"

"White goes with everything," I replied.

Matt flashed a smirky, flirty smile.

"So, what's up?"

"Have you talked to Sophie?" Alex asked. "Does she want to go to the party?"

"She's still deciding." I heard Ginny's voice coming

from the back. "If you wait a minute, you can ask her yourself."

Ginny emerged from the dressing room, followed by Sophie. I don't know who was more amazed at the sight of the other, Alex or Sophie.

"Nice dress!" Matt complimented Sophie.

The silk and slender pearls were as shimmering and delicate as Sophie herself. Her upswept hair showed off her high cheekbones and long neck. The aquamarine pendant was the same misty blue as her eyes. Neither Alex nor Matt could stop looking at her.

"Sophie," Alex said, "for a minute I didn't know you. You, uh, you've grown up."

She frowned. "Since math class? You saw me in math today, remember?"

"Oh, yeah." He reddened. "I guess it's the dress and all."

"No," Ginny corrected him, "it's the *girl* in the dress and all. Okay, honey, let's get your picture over here."

Alex, for once, had been left speechless, so Matt took care of their mission. "Are we on for tomorrow night?" he asked Sophie.

She glanced at me.

"It's your call," I said.

She smiled. "Sure."

Matt volunteered to drive and arranged pickup times, then the guys left. I watched Ginny pose Sophie, thinking that if her camera could catch the glow on Sophie's face, it was a sure sale.

When Sophie had changed back into her school clothes, I took a break and walked her over to the Mallard. As soon as we were on the street, I told her about my conversation with Mrs. Riley.

"It's starting to really scare me, Sophie," I said. "I wake up in a room—I guess I sleepwalked—and find out it was Avril's. Things are moved to where they were when Avril was alive. I dream of a place I've never seen, then see it for real—the mill where Avril and Thomas used to meet, where she went the night she died. I feel like she's haunting me."

"I wonder why she'd choose you," Sophie mused, "other than the fact that you may be psychic," she added slyly.

"I think it's happening to Grandmother, too. I know the relocation of things is getting to her."

"And Matt?"

"He knows something he's not telling me. And he wants me to leave."

We were standing in front of the window of Tea Leaves. Jamie passed by inside and waved to us.

"Did Miss Lydia say anything about how Avril died?" Sophie asked.

When I recounted both versions of the event, Sophie's eyes lit up. "Maybe Avril is trying to set the story straight. There are lots of stories of murder victims haunting people and places until the truth is known."

"The death was an accident," I reminded her.

"Maybe," she replied, and walked on to a bench in front of the Mallard.

I sat down with her. There was one thing I'd been holding off telling her, and I needed to get it out.

"I saw the ghost."

Her eyes opened wide. "You did? When? Where?"

"A couple nights ago, in the upstairs hall. I saw her in the mirror."

Sophie got a funny look on her face. "In the mirror?"

I nodded. "She looked like a mist."

Sophie gazed down at the sidewalk, tracing the shape of a brick with her toe. "Have you ever seen her outside the mirror?"

"No, but I saw her only once."

"When you passed the mirror," Sophie said.

"Ye-ah . . ." She was making me uneasy. "What is it?"

"Megan, the way you talked about your dreams, I thought you were seeing the future or tapping into your mother's past. But maybe that's not it. What if you've been remembering places and objects that you saw in your own past?"

"What do you mean?"

"What if you're Avril—reincarnated?"

I pulled back. "Now you're getting weird."

"It makes sense," she argued. "When you returned to your old house, you instinctively went to your old room. You put your clock back where you kept it. Since the mill was important to you, you noticed a painting of it that seemed out of place."

"Are you saying I moved those things?"

"While you were sleepwalking," Sophie replied. "It probably happened more than once."

I shook my head.

"Avril died when she was a teen," Sophie went on, "and that makes it all the more likely. Reincarnation is a chance to complete what's unfinished in a previous life. For instance, if two lovers—"

"I've seen the movies and know what it is," I said, cutting her off. "A woman gets hypnotized, then remembers bizarre stuff from another century. I'm just having dreams."

"They're the same thing," she replied, "memories buried in the unconscious. They come out in different ways, that's all. Sometimes when a person has experienced a tragic death, there is a symptom of it in the next life. Say a girl died in a fire. In her next life, just seeing a candle being lit might frighten her. Her phobia comes from a memory buried in the unconscious."

"Well, I don't have any phobias," I told Sophie. "And besides, if Avril's spirit was reincarnated, I don't see how she could have a ghost."

"Maybe there isn't one."

"I saw her with my own eyes!"

"In a mirror," Sophie pointed out. "Maybe you had an out-of-body experience and saw your own spirit. Which is what others have been seeing just before dawn. That, too, makes sense—living in a different time zone, your sleep cycle is later than ours."

"No," I insisted.

"Think about the night you saw the mist in the mirror. Do you remember at any point looking down on yourself, looking upon your body as it is now?"

My spine tingled. "At the very end I—I thought I saw myself lying dead."

"Like the way people describe a near-death experience?" she asked. "Like when someone whose heart has stopped sees himself lying on an operating room table?"

I nodded slowly.

"It's an out-of-body experience."

"Or a dream," I replied stubbornly.

Sophie sighed and got up from the bench. "I've got to work. Talk to Miss Lydia. She'll help you understand."

I stood up. "There's nothing to understand."

She laid a hand on my arm. "Megan, listen to me. Sometimes a premature death keeps you from doing the work you were meant to do. Sometimes it separates two people meant to be together. Reincarnation isn't something to fear, it's a second chance."

"I never asked for a second chance."

"Okay, let me put it this way. Do you want the dreams to stop?"

"I want it *all* to stop."

"Then accept the possibility of reincarnation. Find out who you are and what you're to do with your second chance. Once you have, the past will let go of you."

I didn't know what to think. I wasn't the kind to run away from something, and I certainly wanted the strange things that had been happening to end.

"See you tomorrow," she said softly, then went inside.

I walked down High Street and sat for a long time by the water. I knew that Grandmother was more than cold to me—she was jealous. Matt seemed confused, torn between protecting her and defending the time he spent with me. I, for some crazy reason, actually cared about Grandmother. And I was trying to overcome an attraction to Matt that I didn't want to admit. The parallels between the past and present were eerie. Were the three of us playing out parts in a triangle that had existed sixty years ago?

thirteen

I wasn't ready to talk to Mrs. Riley Wednesday afternoon and didn't ask Grandmother why she had gone to see her. Obviously, she was feeling haunted. Questioning her would only make her more hostile toward me. That night I tossed and turned in bed. I discovered the one advantage to lack of sleep: lack of dreams. Still, my mind raced with thoughts as strange as dreams.

If Matt were Thomas, then he must have held me once, he must have kissed me. I quickly squelched that daydream. According to Mrs. Riley, there were a lot of girls in Thomas's life before he settled on Avril. It occurred to me that his love for Avril was not a proven fact. Mrs. Riley told me what she believed at the time, but for all she knew, Thomas may have been planning to break things off with Avril the night she had died. He and Avril might have had a terrible fight. Perhaps the negative feelings from that time had carried over; it sure seemed as if Matt had set his mind against me before we met.

By eight-fifteen Thursday evening I had spun so many theories in my head I didn't know what I thought about Thomas and Avril. But my belief in the possibility that Matt and I had been reincarnated waned: The two of us meant for each other in a previous lifetime? No. He and I were nothing more than a pair of high school kids, cousins who occasionally got along, heading for a party. We set off in his Jeep to pick up Alex and Sophie.

"I hope Kristy won't mind Sophie and me coming," I said, when we stopped at a red light.

"She told us we could bring whoever we wanted," Matt replied. "Which doesn't mean she'll be nice," he added. "But you can handle her."

"Of course I can," I said, which made him laugh. "It's Sophie I'm worried about."

"I'll look out for her," he assured me.

We picked up Alex by the college.

"Stay where you are, Megan," he told me as he climbed in the back. "It's a short ride to Sophie's."

She lived on Shipwrights Street, in the middle of a block of small wooden houses, each one two stories high, two windows wide, with a porch spanning the front. Their tiny yards were neatly hemmed with picket fences.

As soon as we drove up, Sophie came out, followed by her three younger sisters, the oldest of whom looked about nine. The trio lined up on the porch steps to watch.

"Girls," we heard a voice coming from the house. "Gi-irls."

They made stretchy faces and slowly trooped back inside. Meanwhile, Alex had run around the Jeep to open doors.

"Hey, Sophie," I greeted her, about to climb out of the front seat so she could sit there.

I saw her hesitate.

"Oh, yeah," Alex said. "I forgot about that. Megan, do you mind riding up front?"

I looked at him surprised.

"Or I can," he offered.

When I saw Sophie blushing, I quickly pulled in my feet. "No problem."

As soon as she and Alex were settled in the back-seat, she leaned forward. "Sorry, it scares me a little up there."

"Don't blame you, the way Matt drives," I replied.

Matt glanced sideways at me, one side of his mouth curling up. "Sophie," he said as we drove off, "have you been to Kristy's new house?"

"No. I heard it's awesome."

"It's got bathtubs big enough to row across," Alex said.

"Deep enough to drop a trot line?" Sophie asked.

He laughed. "No, it's nice, but not perfect. Hey, guess what I noticed tonight while getting dressed?"

"I don't think I want to," Matt quipped.

"Your valentine," Alex said to Sophie. "I had it tacked inside the door of my bedroom closet. You know, the card with the crab legs drawn around the heart and a boat oar going through it?"

She gazed at him, speechless, then turned to look at me.

"I was wrong," I told her. "I suppose one in a million guys are sentimental."

"Did I miss something?" Matt asked.

"How many things would you like me to list?" I replied.

He rested a hand on mine. "Glad you decided not to be on your good behavior tonight. I wouldn't know what to do with you."

I didn't answer. I was too aware of how his hand felt touching mine.

"You actually saved my valentine?" Sophie said to Alex.

"Is it too late to apologize for being a jerky fifth grader?"

Her voice was gentle. "You weren't jerky, just a fifth grader, a fifth-grade boy."

"How come you don't hang around with Kristy anymore?" Alex asked.

"I don't have the time," she replied. "I help Mom with her job and take care of my sisters. After Mom and Ron had Jenny, I couldn't do all the things Kristy wanted to do. And with Kristy, you're either in or out. I'm out."

They continued to talk, catching up on news about his family and hers.

"Okay, guys, I'm going to need some help finding the turnoff," Matt said.

Only our headlights brightened the dark country road.

"It's about a half mile beyond Dead Man's Curve," Alex told him.

Dead *Woman's*, I thought, remembering Evie's annoyance with the name of the place where Angel Cayton had died.

I glanced back and saw Alex reach for Sophie's hand. It wasn't a friendly pat. He intertwined his fingers with hers and moved closer.

Matt glanced in the rearview mirror. "You taking two dates to the party, Alex?" he asked lightly.

"No, just getting beyond this curve."

"It's always scared me," Sophie explained.

"When we used to ride our bikes down here to fish," Alex said, "she'd make me go the long way so we wouldn't have to take the curve."

We started around the bend, which began slowly, then sharply doubled back on itself. I looked over my shoulder and saw Sophie close her eyes.

"Thanks, Al," she murmured when the road straightened out again.

I stared at her wonderingly. I had been so caught up in Thomas and Avril, I hadn't thought about anyone else from their time. Avril's best friend had been Angel, and Angel had died on the curve that Sophie feared to the point of being phobic. Sophie said she felt a "connection" with me. Was it an old friendship she sensed? Angel had lost her love in the war, so she and Sam Tighe were another case of a couple separated too soon.

I felt surrounded by ghosts, trapped in the events of the past.

"Are you okay?" Matt asked.

When Sophie didn't answer, I did. "She's fine."

"I was talking to you."

I glanced up at him. "Me? Why wouldn't I be?"

"Megan," he said gently, "look at your hands."

I did, then made them lie quiet in my lap.

"I didn't think my driving was *that* bad," he remarked.

"Here it is," Alex called from the backseat.

The turn off took us all the way down to Wist Creek. By the time I climbed out of the Jeep, I'd pulled myself together.

Kristy's house was huge with long sloping roofs, wide wooden beams, and amazing spans of glass. The four of us walked into a two-story foyer lit by a globe chandelier.

"Hey, guys! Come on in," Kristy called, her voice carrying from another room. Then she came through the archway and saw Sophie and me. For a long moment she didn't say anything—she didn't have to. The dramatic way she stopped and blinked her eyes let us know she couldn't believe that we had come.

"Well, hello. This is a surprise."

"I told you we were bringing dates," Matt said.

"Yes, but you didn't—well, never mind."

Didn't say you were bringing *them,* I filled in the blanks.

"Come on, party's in the back. I haven't seen you for such a long time, Sophie," Kristy said and took her by the arm.

Alex and Matt waited for me.

The party, which started in the kitchen and family room, where Kristy's parents were, spread to a wide double-level deck, then spilled out on the lawn below, ending at the dock on the creek. Music blasted from the deck and groups of kids sat on blankets in the grass. It was all pretty laid back.

When Alex and I stopped to talk to some kids on the deck steps, Matt moved on with Sophie and Kristy. Alex introduced me to a guy and girl who had camped in Colorado and loved white-water rafting as much as I did, and after that, a girl who worked for a vet and wanted to be one. It would have been a great party if I hadn't had so many strange ideas and questions running through my mind—and if it hadn't been Kristy's.

"You're frowning," Alex observed, his eyes following mine.

I was watching Kristy. "You'd think she was Sophie's best friend," I said indignantly. "But I know what she's doing. She's using Sophie, and then she's going to ditch her. All Kristy wants to do is flirt with Matt."

"That's all a lot of girls want to do," Alex replied with a smile. We walked down the hill toward the creek. "How about you?"

"How about me what?"

"Are you interested in Matt?" he asked.

"He's my cousin."

"Sort of," Alex reminded me.

My laugh sounded fake. I quickly changed the subject. "Want to go out on the dock?"

"You're asking me? The closer to the water, the better," he said.

We walked to the end, about thirty feet offshore. The dock's pilings were lit with small lights that drew lavender circles on the dark water.

I asked Alex about catching crabs, about how you chicken neck and set a trot line, the things that Sophie had mentioned.

"You and Sophie really hit it off," he observed, sounding happy about it.

I nodded. "I've known her only a couple days, but it seems like we've always been friends."

I couldn't believe that had popped out of my mouth. Coincidence, I told myself; you're reading into things.

"She can be the best friend in the world," Alex replied fervently, then gazed in her direction.

She and Matt were standing by a table beneath a string of colored lanterns. Sophie talked and Matt bent his head, smiling, listening intently to her. For a moment I wondered what it would be like to have

Matt smiling at me, as entranced as he seemed right then. I snuffed out that thought. Sophie was interested in Matt, and if the two of them got together, it would be the best thing that could happen.

At that moment Kristy moved in. Talk about rude! There were three guys standing close by, waiting to help her set up food, but apparently it was Matt's help that she wanted–Matt's attention.

Alex threw his head back and laughed. "Megan, if you were a cat, your back would be arched and your fur standing on end."

I grimaced. "My father says I wear my heart on my sleeve."

"No, just your thoughts," Alex replied softly. "It's pretty easy to guess what you're thinking. But your heart, you keep that hidden."

"Sometimes even I'm not sure what's there," I admitted.

He smiled and gave me a friendly hug. "Whatever it is, I'm sure it's okay."

When Alex let go, I saw that Matt was staring at us.

"Hey, they're putting out food," Alex said. "Stay where you are. I'll get some and we'll have a picnic out here."

"Great!"

He started off and I turned away from the party to gaze out at the creek. With a late-rising moon and no street lamps nearby, the stars were brilliant. Close to the dock the water rippled, then lay quiet again, hiding the creatures that moved beneath its surface. The darkness was beautiful; the secrets it held, enticing.

A few minutes later I heard Alex coming back.

"I wish I could visit here in the summer," I said, "and swim in the creek at night."

"Do you?"

I turned around quickly when I heard his voice. "I thought you were Alex!"

Matt gazed long and hard at me. "He'll be back. I came out to let you know that Sophie is having a good time, so you can stop worrying. You can stop watching her."

"I guess I'm being obvious."

"I told you I'd look out for her," he said.

"I'm glad she's having fun. She's really nice and really pretty and, uh, Matt, mind if I give you some advice?"

"You're going to anyway."

"I know you're like—well—the main heartthrob of your school."

His expression changed. He seemed surprised, then amused. "Really," he said.

"I know you can have any girl you want."

"I can? I wish someone had told me that before. *Any* girl?" He took a step toward me. We were standing close, too close, but I couldn't step back—there was no dock left behind me. "Anyone at this party?"

"Well, just about," I told him.

"Wait a minute," he said. "A moment ago there weren't limits."

"Don't be greedy. My point is, there's Sophie." I gestured toward the shore, but he kept his eyes on me. "She likes you. She's gorgeous—I mean you must have noticed yesterday at the shop."

"I can see."

"Obviously, Kristy is, too. Gorgeous, I mean."

He tilted his head to one side, frowning.

"The point is Sophie is not only pretty, like some girls, she is also nice, friendly, sweet, and—"

"Not my type," he said.

"*And,*" I continued, undeterred, "she doesn't have a mouth."

His gaze dropped down to my mouth. I glanced to the side. When I looked back, he was still gazing at me, his eyes dark and mysterious as the creek. His lips parted slightly. He looked so long and so steadily at my mouth, my cheeks burned and heart pounded. I felt his eyes making my lips soft. I felt as if his eyes were kissing me.

"Not like yours," he agreed, then turned and walked back to shore.

fourteen

or the rest of the party I was careful not to look at Matt and Sophie, but Alex picked up where I had left off. I wondered if he was becoming interested in his best old friend. The ride home was awkward, our conversation mostly dumb cracks about Kristy's house. After dropping off Alex and Sophie, Matt and I rode in silence.

I was aware of his every movement, the way he shifted in his seat, how his hand rested on the steering wheel. Why did I respond to him so strongly? Even when Matt was his most obnoxious, the day I met him, his eyes had cast a spell on me. Had we once been in love? Was I falling for him a second time?

At home I thanked him for the ride and headed for the refuge of my room.

Having slept little the night before, I drifted off as

soon as I lay down. When my eyes opened again, the sky was beginning to lighten. I heard the chime of the clock on the stairway landing and counted the hours—five, six, seven—I turned over—eight, nine, ten—couldn't be—eleven, twelve, thirteen. Silence.

My digital alarm read 5:00 A.M. I listened for a moment, then climbed out of bed and tiptoed to the door of my room. Opening it, I saw the stairwell was lit from below. I crept down the steps to the landing and gazed at the clock's pale face. Its hands pointed to a few minutes after midnight. In the window above the numbers, the picture of the moon was halfway up.

Using the key, I opened the glass door that protected its face. Though I could hear the clock ticking, its hands didn't move. With the tip of one finger, I tried to push the large hand forward. It would not move, so I eased it counterclockwise till the clock read a few minutes after five. I thought I had set things right, then I noticed the small second-hand dial in the clock's face. Its wand flicked backward over each lash of a second. Ever so slowly the clock's minute hand moved in reverse. Time was turning in the wrong direction.

I stepped back, afraid, and teetered on the edge of the landing. Strong hands gripped my arms and pulled me back to safety.

"It's only a clock," he said.

"Thomas!"

We were standing close, close enough to kiss, but I

couldn't step away from him. If his hands hadn't held me, his dark eyes would have.

"I hate that clock," I said. "It is always telling us what to do when."

Thomas laughed. "And you certainly don't want to do what is expected of you."

"Do you?" I asked.

"I used to." His gaze dropped to my mouth. He looked so long, so steadily, my cheeks burned and my heart pounded. I felt his eyes making my lips soft. I felt as if they were kissing me.

"April," he whispered, "I can't stop thinking of you."

I didn't say a word—I knew the pain we could cause. But every time he looked at me, every time he spoke his special name for me, I wanted him more.

He laid his hand against my cheek, then touched my mouth with one finger, running it over my lip.

Just once, I thought, gazing up at him. One kiss wouldn't be so terribly wrong.

He bent his head and our mouths moved closer. His lips brushed my cheek, the lightest touch of him making me shiver. Then his arms tightened around me, and I felt the warmth and tenderness of his lips against mine.

"Thomas!"

We both pulled back. My sister stood at the top of the stairs glaring down at us.

Thomas let go of me. "Helen, I—"

"Don't try to explain," she told him angrily. "Don't make it any worse for me. Leave, Thomas."

"But I need to explain," he said. "I've let things go too long."

"Leave!" she shouted. "Now!"

He looked at me and I nodded.

"I–I'm very sorry," he told her.

My sister waited till Thomas was gone, then started toward me, her eyes burning with anger. "Is there nothing of mine you don't want, Avril?" she asked. "Is there nothing of mine you won't take for yourself?"

I bit my lip.

"Mama and Papa already give you whatever you ask for."

I closed my eyes, knowing what was coming next.

"The servants will do anything for you. Your friends cover for you. All the boys in this town wait on you."

"Helen, it's not my fault that—" I broke off.

"That you're everyone's favorite?" she finished for me. Her face was so pale, her skin so tight, I could see the bones moving beneath it. "Say it, Avril, it's the truth."

I looked away.

"You have everything. Did you have to take Thomas, too?"

"I can't help the way I feel about him," I said. "He can't help the way he feels about me."

"And what about good old Helen?" she asked. "Does it matter at all what I feel?"

Her eyes were bloodshot. I knew she was trying not to cry. My heart felt cut in two. I ached for her, but I ached for us as well.

"Do you think because I keep my emotions in check that I feel nothing?"

I was desperate to prove myself right. "If two people feel the same way about each other," I reasoned, "then that must matter more than what one person feels."

"I can't believe you'd do this to me!" she cried, her voice quivering with anger. "One day you're going to pay, Avril."

She took a step toward me, then another. Something in Helen had shattered, the lock she kept on her fierce passion had been broken. I could see the fury in her eyes, in the curl of her fingers.

"Mark my words," she said, coming toward me. "You're going to pay."

I stepped back quickly and missed my footing. I reached out, but couldn't stop the fall. My head snapped back and I tumbled downward, the edge of each tread banging against my spine. I heard Helen scream—scream as she did when we were children, "I didn't mean it! I didn't mean it!"

Then everything went black.

"Megan! Are you all right?"

My back hurt and my arm, jammed against the stairway banister, buzzed with pain. Matt knelt next to me, halfway down the flight of steps.

"Just a little bruised," I answered shakily.

He helped me sit up. "What happened?"

"I'm not sure." I struggled to put together the jumbled images in my mind. "I must have been sleep-walking. I did it a few nights ago. You didn't see me fall?"

"I was in the library," he said. "When I heard the noise, I rushed out and found you here."

"What time is it?"

He glanced over my shoulder. "About ten after five."

I turned to look at the clock on the landing and suddenly remembered the thirteen chimes and the scene with Avril, Helen, and Thomas. This time I wasn't dreaming simply of a place, but an event. Had it actually happened? Was I fantasizing, elaborating on the story that Mrs. Riley had told me, or was I truly remembering?

Until Matt touched my cheek, I hadn't realized I was crying. "What's wrong?" he asked. "Tell me." He gently took my face in his hands.

I didn't know how to begin to explain. "It was so real," I whispered. "But that's what crazy people always think, that what they imagine is real."

He put his arms around me and pulled me close. I buried my face between his neck and shoulder.

"You're not crazy." He smoothed my hair. "I promise you, you're not."

"I—I've had a lot of weird dreams since I've come here."

"Dreams about what?" he asked softly.

"Places, people. Thomas, Avril, and Helen—Grand-mother. Dreams about the past."

His arms tightened around me. I could hear his heart beating fast.

"Were you dreaming when you fell?" he asked.

"Yes."

"Tell me about it."

"In the dream Grandmother was young, no older than us. And she was furious with her sister. She had walked in on Avril and Thomas."

I felt him swallow hard.

"They were kissing."

The motion was slight, but I sensed it, the way he pulled back from me.

"Grandmother threatened Avril," I added, then the tears streamed down my face again.

"Megan, you should leave."

"Leave?" That's not what I wanted to hear from him, not now that I was wrapped in his arms. "Why?"

"I think that if you leave, all of this will stop."

"All of this meaning what?" I asked.

"You know what."

Suddenly I wasn't in his arms anymore; he had let go and stood up. "Come on, I want to show you something."

Matt led me to the library, where the lamp on Grandmother's desk was already lit, and gestured for me to sit in her chair. After retrieving a key from a vase on the mantel, he returned to the desk and unlocked a drawer.

"I saw you in here," I told him, "the first night I came."

He laid several flat boxes on the desk in front of me. "I was looking at these. Have you ever seen a picture of Aunt Avril?"

"No."

"She's pretty." He lifted a lid and handed me a black-and-white photo. "Look like anyone you know?"

My breath caught. Her resemblance to me was striking.

He opened another box. "There's a colorized photo in here, a portrait." He sorted through the pictures, then handed one to me.

"Gray eyes," I observed. "Her hair's lighter than mine, but her eyes are gray and the facial structure's the same."

"You see why Grandmother is going crazy," Matt said. "You look like her sister. You look like Avril the year she died, and it's spooking her."

I nodded. "The question is why. Sixty years is too long to be mourning a sister, to be upset about seeing someone who resembles her . . . unless there is more to the story."

I looked at him expectantly, but he said nothing.

"In my dream Grandmother told Avril she would pay for what she had done."

"So?"

"What did she mean by that?"

"Sounds like a typical fight between sisters," he replied, but he wouldn't meet my eyes. He knew more than he was saying.

"Mrs. Riley said the cause of death was an overdose."

His hand tensed till it creased the picture he held. What had Grandmother told him the night they had spoken in her bedroom?

"But," I continued, "who would know the difference between an accidental overdose and deliberate poisoning?"

"You can't be thinking—"

"Only Avril," I continued, "and the person who poisoned her, the murderer, if there is one."

"Megan, I told you not to trust Lydia. She makes her money off people's fears. She suggests things and lets people make themselves crazy wondering about them."

"So, why did Grandmother go to see her the other day?"

"You'll have to ask her," he said brusquely. His face was a mask. Grandmother had nothing to worry about—he wasn't telling her secrets. I was the one who should be wary of what I said to him; he probably told *her* everything.

"Does that key work on the other drawers?" I asked.

He unlocked them, and I started going through files and boxes.

"Look at these." I showed him photos of myself and my brothers, our names and ages inscribed on the back in my mother's handwriting. Grandmother never even sent us a Christmas card, but apparently my mother kept writing to her, kept trying to make contact.

Matt placed a picture of me on the first day of kindergarten next to a young one of Avril, then shook his head slowly. He cradled in his hand a photo of Avril standing by the gate in the herb garden. "It's scary how much you look alike."

"It's as if I've been here before," I said, watching his face carefully. "Have you ever felt like that, Matt, like you've been in this house some time long before now?"

"No," he answered quickly.

Perhaps I was reading into it, but it seemed to me that if Matt had never thought about reincarnation, my question would have drawn a different response, a slower one. He would have looked at me puzzled and asked what I meant.

"You should leave," he said.

"No way."

"Why are you so stubborn?" he exclaimed.

"It's you who are stubbornly refusing to open your mind to questions and explanations you don't like. I'm staying here till I find out what's going on."

"Nothing's going on," he argued, walking away from me. "You look like Avril. It's just a bad coincidence, and you're going to make both yourself and Grandmother insane over it." He started pacing the room.

"Did you move any of the objects in this house?" I asked.

Matt swung around. "I'm not the kind to play tricks."

"Then you must suspect me," I said. "But think about it. How would I know where those objects were kept when Avril was alive, unless—"

"Grandmother moved them," he interrupted. "Maybe she's gotten senile and did it without remembering, or this is just some crazy spell she'll snap out of. Whatever the case, you're not making things any easier for her."

He walked over to me. "Finished?" Without waiting for my answer, he put the photos and boxes back in the drawers and turned the key in the lock.

"Matt, those pictures mean that Grandmother has always known that I look like her sister. She knew and chose to invite me. I want to know why."

"Curiosity," he replied.

"Guilt," I countered. "Morbid curiosity and guilt."

Matt shook his head. "You're getting stranger than Grandmother. Take my advice, Megan. Get out of here. Get out before it's too late for both of you."

I got up from my chair. "Sorry. It already is."

fifteen

When I returned to my room, I couldn't get back to sleep, so I dressed and took a long walk, spending time by the water then stopping by Avril's grave. It didn't give me the same eerie feeling as the first time I saw it. Perhaps seeing your own grave is like looking at a gushing wound on your leg: Once you're over the initial shock, it seems natural enough. I knelt down before the stone and traced the name and dates with my finger. On the final date my finger stopped. Today. Avril had died sixty years ago today.

When I finally arrived back at the house, it was nine o'clock. I entered through the front hall, wanting to avoid Grandmother and Matt in the kitchen. I was angry with Matt for turning away when I needed his help. He had chosen Grandmother over me, determined to protect her at any cost.

I crept upstairs, stuffed some things in a backpack, and headed out again, leaving a note in the hall telling Grandmother I'd be gone for a while. My first stop was the library at Chase College. I hoped to access local newspaper articles from Avril's time that might shed light on what had happened.

Three hours later, totally frustrated by the library's ancient and cranky microfiche machines, I'd found just one short piece on Avril that attributed her death to allergic reaction. It made no mention of the mill or Thomas. After trying a number of sources on red-creep, it became obvious that its local name would not yield information on the plant and its by-products. But I got lucky with Angel Cayton. She had not only started the Watermen's Fund but contributed to the college. A librarian directed me to a conference room where her portrait hung.

Angel looked like all the other matrons honored in the conference room, with gray hair, blue eyes, and a bustline that could amply support pearls and eye-glasses—only she wasn't wearing pearls. Around her neck hung a silver chain with a blue gem as mystical as the eyes of my newest—and perhaps oldest—friend. It was the pendant Sophie loved.

I opened the front gate. "Is Sophie around?" I called to the group of little girls who were playing dolls on the porch. Barbie and Ken kissed with loud smacking noises, then one of Sophie's sisters turned to me. "Mom said we can only have one friend over at a time. Sophie's already got one."

"I'll be just a minute. Is she inside?"

"Around back," said another sister.

I followed a stone path to the narrow space between the Quinns' house and the house next door and emerged into a backyard.

"Oh," I said, though I shouldn't have been surprised. "Hi."

Sophie, who had been leaning over a tub of suds, leaped to her feet. A large black-and-white dog jumped with her. Alex caught the dog just before it escaped its bath. Soap bubbles flurried around them.

"Hey, Megan," Alex said, smiling. "Want to help us wash Rose? We'll throw in a free bath for you."

I laughed. "Thanks, but I've already had mine. I'll watch."

"Rose met up with a skunk this morning," Sophie told me.

"I'll watch from a distance."

"And Alex sort of stopped by to help," she continued, looking embarrassed.

"Glad he got here first," I teased.

"It was nice because he hadn't seen the girls for a while," she added, as if Alex had come by with the passionate hope that he could deskunk her dog and visit her sisters.

"Like I told you before, we're just old friends."

She was so worried that she was intruding on my

dating territory, she missed the expression on Alex's face—the protest he almost spoke aloud. I saw it and smiled.

"You know, Sophie, I'm here for a two-week visit," I reminded her. "And I doubt Grandmother will be asking me back."

Alex realized that I was giving Sophie "permission" to go with whomever she wanted and glanced sideways at her, but she didn't get it. I don't think it had crossed her mind that her old crabbing buddy was falling for her—falling fast, I'd say.

"How's Matt today?" Alex asked.

"Hot and bothered, thanks to me."

"Any chance of you two cutting each other a break?" he asked.

"Don't think so," I replied, and tried to ignore the ache inside me.

I watched him and Sophie work the soap through the thick fur of the dog, debating what to say in front of Alex. How aware was he of Sophie's psychic side? He seemed an open-minded person; still, I decided to mention only what I had to.

"Listen, Sophie, I'm trying to get information on the plant called redcreep. Do you know its botanical name?"

"No, but Miss Lydia might."

"What do you need to know about it?" Alex asked.

"I was told that people used it as a beauty supplement. I want to know if the processed stuff has any taste—or smell or color. Does it dissolve in liquid?

What exactly does it do to you? How fast does it work? How much is too much and what are the symptoms of an overdose—uh, you know, that kind of thing," I added casually, after giving a list that belonged in a forensic lab.

"Why do you want to know?" he asked.

I glanced at Sophie.

"It's a long story," she answered for me. "How about someone at the college, Alex—would one of the biology profs know?"

"We can find out," he replied.

"Would you?" I asked quickly. "I've got some other things to do. Thanks. I'll catch up with you later." I started across the grass.

"Megan," Sophie called, hurrying after me. "Megan!" She waited till we were in the side yard, out of earshot. "What are you up to?"

"I have a lot to tell you," I said, "but not now. I want to talk to Mrs. Riley, then go to the mill."

"Don't."

"Don't what?"

"Go to the mill. I have a bad feeling about it." Shaded by a cedar, her blue eyes were a flicker of light and shadow.

"Look, Sophie, don't get prophetic on me. It's the past I need info on, not the future."

"I'm telling you, it's dangerous."

"I'll watch where I step and look out for rodents."

"You're asking for it," she warned.

"Is that a prediction?"

"Yes."

"Want to hear my prediction?"

She looked surprised, then smiled. "From the person who claims she isn't psychic? Okay."

"Before I leave Wisteria, you and Alex are going to be totally in love."

I left Sophie with a look of wonder on her face.

Mrs. Riley couldn't see me. At first I suspected that the purpose of Grandmother's visit had been to forbid the woman to speak to me, then I saw the worry on Jamie's face.

"She's had another bad night and is resting now. How about I fix you a late lunch? Some dessert?"

"No, thanks." Though I hadn't eaten that morning, I had no appetite.

"Try back later," he said. "I'm sure she'll feel better."

I wandered up and down the streets of Wisteria, hoping for inspiration, some theory about what had happened sixty years ago that would help me understand what was going on now. Each time I tried to reject the idea of reincarnation, I came back to it. It was the one theory that explained all the strange things that had been happening. Sophie's suggestion made sense: While sleepwalking I had moved the Bible, the clock, and the painting to where they belonged when I was Avril. Small matters fell into place, such as Matt's reluctance to go to the mill. Did he remember something terrible happening there? Was he trying to get me away from Wisteria before I remembered?

On my wanderings I passed Tea Leaves, and Jamie flagged me down. He said his mother wanted to see me at four. I used the remaining time to look for Sophie, checking her house and Alex's, then the college, but didn't catch up with her. I browsed in a New Age bookstore, looking at covers and reading their fantastic blurbs, till the incense and tinkling music got to me—not to mention the weird shoppers.

They're probably all Mrs. Riley's patrons, I thought; and now I'm one of them.

At four o'clock the old woman was waiting for me, beckoning from the top of the café stairway. I climbed it and followed her down the narrow hall. When we sat at the table beneath the fringed lamp, I saw the deep circles under her eyes. There was a tremor on one side of her mouth that I hadn't noticed before. She lay her palms flat on the table in front of her. Her fingers looked sore, the nails bitten down to the pink.

"What is it you want of me?" she asked.

I hesitated, torn between my own need to get answers and the realization that she wasn't well.

"You want to know more about Avril and Helen," she guessed.

"You look so tired," I said, starting to rise.

"Stay!" She gripped my wrist with surprising strength. "I have been concerned about you and hoping to see you again. Ask your questions."

I sat down and carefully pulled away my hand, lowering it into my lap. "I want to find out about reincarnation."

"Go on."

"Sophie told me it's a chance to complete things that have been left undone."

Mrs. Riley nodded.

"She said that if a person died young, she might be reincarnated. Sometimes two people can be reincarnated together if they are separated too soon in a previous life."

Mrs. Riley studied my face. "And you think that has happened to you?"

"I think I'm Avril."

The old woman sat back in her chair. After a moment she said, "Do not be misled by appearances. You look like your great aunt, but that is not significant."

"It's not what I look like. It's what I dream about. It's what I seem to remember."

The shrill whistle of a teakettle sounded in another room. Mrs. Riley ignored it.

"What do you remember?" she whispered.

"Scarborough House. The dollhouse that looks like it. I dreamed about them before I saw them."

"And?" she asked, her eyes as bright and sharp as the whistling sound.

"The mill, its basement, the big wheels in it."

"And?" she pressed.

I bit my lip. "That's it." The dream about Thomas, Helen, and Avril was too uncomfortable, too personal to tell.

She looked at me doubtfully. "You must be honest with me if I am to help you."

I stared down at the table and said nothing.

She stood up. "Very well. Think about it while I get my tea."

As soon as she disappeared, I covered my face with my hands. What did I hope to prove—that Grandmother was guilty? Why reveal that now? It would only cause a lot of pain. Still, the doubt and suspicion that grew out of that dark secret were quietly poisoning the minds of Grandmother, Matt, and me.

Mrs. Riley reentered the room and set two cups on the table. "It's cinnamon apple."

"Thank you," I said, then sipped the fragrant tea.

"Do you know anything about karma?" she asked.

"I've heard of it."

"It is the belief that we are rewarded or punished in one life according to our deeds in a previous life." She held her cup in both hands and gazed at her tea as if reading it, then took a long drink. "Karma is just," she said. "According to it, the victim of an unnatural death will return in a later life and seek out the killer."

"Seek out the killer?" I repeated.

"It's justice, dear. If you take away someone's life, then in the next cycle, your life will be taken by that person. The victim will kill the murderer."

I stared at her. Did she know what I suspected?

"You're remembering, aren't you," she said quietly.

I sipped my tea, avoiding her eyes.

"What is it?" she asked, her voice soothing. "Avril, tell me what you are remembering."

"I had a dream," I said at last. "Helen was very angry

at me. She threatened me, said I would pay. But that doesn't mean anything," I added quickly. "Brothers and sisters say that all the time without meaning it."

"True enough," the psychic replied. "Do you remember anything else—anything from the day you died?"

"No."

"And yet you are remembering more and more," she said. "I don't know how to advise you." She rose from the table and walked restlessly around the room. "I have my suspicions. To speak them may influence a clear memory. Not to may endanger you. You know that Helen came to see me yesterday."

I ran my finger around the moist rim of my cup. "Yes."

"I warned you, child, not to tell her you were here."

"But I didn't. Someone in the café must have told her."

"Can you trust your cousin?" Mrs. Riley asked. "You're hesitating. That tells me you can't."

"He's very protective of Grandmother."

Her hands worked nervously. "Then it would be foolish and dangerous to trust him."

"Why?"

"He's loyal to her, dependent on her money, and you fear the same thing I do—that you were murdered by Helen."

For a moment the raw statement of my suspicion shocked me. I struggled to think clearly.

"But if I was the victim in my past life," I reasoned,

"I'm the one who is the threat now. According to karma, Avril would destroy her murderer—that's what you said. And I would never hurt my grandmother."

"The act does not have to be intentional."

"But what if I make sure I don't hurt her?" I argued. "What if I leave and never come back?"

Was that why Matt wanted me to go? Did he know more about this than he pretended?

"Karma is karma," Mrs. Riley responded. "There is only one thing that can prevent the victim from achieving justice."

"What?"

"Her own death."

I looked at her, startled. "You mean, dying a second time? You mean my death?"

"*Now* you understand why you must remember what happened that day. Just because you would not hurt others, doesn't mean others won't hurt you, not when it comes to saving themselves. You must find out your enemy."

My mouth went dry. I felt as if I couldn't breathe. "I can't will myself to remember. I'm not psychic like you or Sophie. I have no control—the dreams come when they want to."

Mrs. Riley came back to the table. "Today is the anniversary of Avril's death," she said, her voice calm, steadying me. "There is a window of time when the past will be open to you. Can you get to the mill?"

"Yes."

"Go straightaway. Walk around it, breathe it, touch

it. Listen to its sounds, let it become part of your life again. Go inside and make yourself quiet there, let the past come back to you. Your life depends on it."

I sat still as a stone.

Her brow creased, then she rested her veined hand gently on mine. "Finish your tea, child, then hurry. You haven't much time if you want to be home before dark."

sixteen

I didn't run fast, but when I reached the mill, I was out of breath and had a stitch in my side. I walked slowly around the building, waiting for the pain to ease, mulling over what I had learned from Mrs. Riley. If Grandmother had murdered Avril, then I, the reincarnated Avril, was destined to take Grandmother's life. Did she know that? When she had gone to see Mrs. Riley, what had they talked about?

Grandmother would never harm me, I told myself. But then I thought, if she murdered her own sister, how hard would it be to do away with a grandchild, an adopted grandchild? With sixty long years in between, another accident would not seem suspicious. And she could count on Matt to protect her.

Matt's attitude toward me had changed in the short time between our first meeting and that moment on the dock. Had he exploited my attraction to him to keep tabs on me?

"Tell me," he'd said later, holding my face gently in his hands, seeming as if he wanted to help. Perhaps all he wanted was information and to keep me from looking further. I was more determined than ever to find out what had happened in this place.

Breathe it, touch it, listen to its sounds, Mrs. Riley had said. I pulled on the long grass, feeling its sharp edges. I took a deep breath and smelled the salty water. The creek lapped gently, slipping between grasses and stones. The birds sounded exceptionally loud and sweet to me. I emptied my mind of everything but the mill and felt as if I were walking in a dream.

Since I had left both basement doors open, I entered the mill easily. I looked across the room at the wheels, then forced myself to go to them, to touch the biggest one. I wrapped my fingers around a metal tooth and gripped it hard. Rusted saws and metal circles that looked like disembodied steering wheels lay here and there. It wasn't a cozy place for two people to meet. The next floor up would be drier and brighter, I thought.

I saw the stairway along one wall, the same as in my dream, like a tilted ladder with wide wooden treads and no handrail. I walked under it and pulled on each step to see if it would support my weight. One split in half and two others cracked, but they were spaced well enough for me to climb to the trapdoor.

When I was near the top of the steps, I pushed

against a square piece of ceiling. The trapdoor was heavier than it looked. I managed to shove it up, swinging it back against a wall, carelessly assuming the door would stay. It slammed down on me. I was stunned by the force and clung to the top step, feeling dizzy. There were small, scurrying sounds—the mill's residents.

Determined to get to the next floor, I pushed against the trapdoor again. Then I grabbed a long piece of wood and placed it diagonally between the floor and the hinged door to prop it open. I climbed through and looked around the first-floor space.

Though the windows were shuttered, crooked seams of light shown through cracks in the plank walls. In one corner of the room was a round iron stove, missing its chimney pipe. Barrels and bins, burlap bags gnawed apart by rats, and frayed rope were strewn about. Narrow chutes built in long rectangular sections with elbow joints looked like the arms of wooden people coming down through the ceiling. The ceiling itself gaped with holes. The trapdoor above the stairs to the second floor appeared to be open. Gazing up into it, I suddenly felt light-headed.

I found a millstone, half of a pair used for grinding, and sat on it. Closing my eyes, I ran my hands over its rough surface, feeling the long, angled ridges. Waves of confused images and sensations washed over me: the sound of voices, Thomas's face, Matt's, the clock chiming, the sound of engines, my name being called, footsteps against a hard surface. I wasn't sure what was inside my mind and what was outside. I couldn't tell what was then and what was now, when I was Avril and when I was Megan. Everything seemed real but distorted, the sounds and images stretched at the edges.

Hunching over, resting my head on my knees, I saw moving lines of light. I struggled to focus.

Light between the floorboards—that was it. Someone with a flashlight was walking downstairs. Did the person know I was here? Instinct told me to hide. I crouched behind a pair of barrels.

Peering around the edge of them, I saw the orb of light dodge its way up the stairs, held by an unsteady hand.

"Child? Are you here? It's Lydia," she whispered as she climbed the last step.

I breathed a sigh of relief.

"I need to talk to you. I have seen something and must warn you."

Before I could emerge, another voice cried out. "Megan! Are you in here?"

It was Matt. At the sound of his voice Mrs. Riley moved quickly, hiding behind a bin.

"Where are you?" Matt called. I heard him walking below us, then hurrying up the steps. "Megan? Answer me!"

His words brought back the memory with sudden force. "Answer me! Answer me, Avril!"

Thomas's hands gripped my shoulders. He shook me so hard my head snapped back. He started dragging me down the mill steps. My chest hurt. It felt like straps of steel had tightened around it. Every breath was agony.

I pushed away from Thomas, gasping, desperate for air. He held me tighter. I tried to speak, but the darkness was closing in on me. I needed air!

I staggered to my feet, grasping the barrels to steady myself. Matt spun around. I was in the present again. I was Megan. But Matt's eyes were identical to Thomas's.

He started toward me.

"Run, child!" Mrs. Riley cried. "Run before he hurts you."

We both turned toward her. The surprise on Matt's face quickly changed to anger.

"Shut up, old woman," he said. "You've done enough."

"I'm not afraid of you," she replied, her eyes bright, challenging the fire in his. "Are you remembering now, Thomas?" she asked. "Are you remembering all of it now?"

"I don't know what you're talking about."

"That's why you came to me three years ago, isn't it?" Mrs. Riley continued. "You were seeing *her* face. She had come back to haunt you."

Matt glanced at me, then back at Mrs. Riley.

"But you didn't think you'd see her in flesh and blood again, did you?" she prodded.

"Your mind is twisted," he said. "It's been twisted for years. You've preyed on my grandmother's fears. You knew she wanted to make Avril sick that night so she couldn't meet Thomas. You gave her the redcreep and told her how much to put in the tea, but she cut that amount in half, and Avril was well enough to go. It was another dose, a later dose, that killed her. Still, you convinced Grandmother that she had given her sister too much, that she was responsible for her death. Grandmother had always been jealous, hurt by the attention Avril received, wishing that Avril would get out of her life. It was easy to change those feelings into guilt. You enjoyed torturing her with false guilt."

"I did enjoy it," Mrs. Riley admitted. "She was so self-righteous. But I believed it, too. I realized a second dose had been given"—her voice softened—"but I was *so* in love with you when you were Thomas."

Matt took a step back from her.

"I was so naive," she continued. "I couldn't believe you had done it. It had to be Helen, I thought. I couldn't accept that my Thomas was a cold-blooded murderer."

He was the murderer? Waves of fear and nausea washed over me. Matt, not Grandmother, was the one who should fear me. Did he know it? I remembered the strange way he had looked at me the day we met. He had known from the beginning.

"I should have realized that it was Helen you wanted all along," Mrs. Riley continued.

Matt's dark eyes burned in his pale face.

"Avril was too unpredictable, too much of a flirt. But the fortune was hers. So you played up to her and killed her, then you and Helen got everything."

His fists clenched.

"Nothing has changed since then," Mrs. Riley

added. "You still depend on Helen's money. You will be loyal to her till the end."

"You're wrong," Matt argued, "dead wrong."

"Even when the other boys would come here to swim," she said, "you couldn't bear to be in this place. You told me so yourself."

"I was an idiot to trust you."

"Karma," Mrs. Riley said softly. "Justice at last. Sixty years ago you wanted nothing to do with me, Thomas, not when you realized you could have the Scarborough girls."

Matt turned his back on her. "She's crazy, Megan. Let's get out of here."

"No." My tongue felt thick in my mouth, and I struggled to speak clearly. "Stay away."

"She's a liar, a troublemaker," Matt said. "I told you that before. You can't believe her."

"I do."

He took two steps toward me. One more and he'd trap me behind the barrels. I moved my hand slowly, then shoved a barrel at him and ran past his grasp.

He whirled around. I faced him, my back to the wall, inching sideways, feeling my way along the rough wood, trying to get to the steps that led down to the basement.

"Listen to me. You're not yourself," he said.

"I know who I am." The words came out slurred. "And who I was. So do you."

He looked at Mrs. Riley. "What have you done to her?"

"I told her about karma," the woman replied. "She knows what you know."

"Megan, come here." He held out his hand. "Come here!"

I shook my head and continued inching sideways.

"You must trust me."

"I trusted you before." My mouth moved slowly, my thoughts and words getting jumbled. "I trusted you when you were Thomas."

Matt's eyes darted around the room. His hands flexed, then he sprang at me. I lurched sideways and scrambled free. But he caught my shirt, yanking me back. Then something hissed and snapped between us. Matt let go, quickly pulling back his hand, burned by the rope Mrs. Riley had brought down like a whip.

I rushed blindly ahead, crashing into a plank of wood, part of the open stairs rising to the next floor. I clung to it. I had to get up. Had to get away from him.

Matt pushed back Mrs. Riley and came after me. "If you won't come, I'll drag you out of here."

I started to climb, but it felt as if the stair, the entire room, was tilting. I could barely hang on.

Matt stood at the bottom, studying me.

"No closer," I said. I didn't want either of us to die.

He put a foot on the bottom plank. "Something's wrong with you, Megan."

"No closer!"

I pulled myself up another step, then another. It was like moving in a dream, climbing in slow motion.

Matt started up the steps, but Mrs. Riley came after

him like a cat. I saw something flash in her hand. Matt dropped backward. He turned and struggled with her, grabbing her wrists. A knife flew across the floor.

"What have you done to her, Lydia?" he demanded.

"Nothing."

"Liar!" he shouted. "You've poisoned her."

The woman fought to get free. He pinned her hands behind her, then turned his face up to me. "Don't run from me, Megan."

I took two more steps up.

"Can't you understand? You need help, medical help. Come down."

There was a pipe propping open the trapdoor. If I could get through the door and close it, I could use my weight to keep it shut.

"Please," Matt said, grasping the ladder with one hand, "don't let Lydia do this to us."

I reached up to pull myself through.

"April!" he cried. "Don't leave me again!"

It was the name he had written on my heart. I turned to look down at him. My foot slipped. Reaching out wildly, I grabbed hold of the pipe that propped open the door. For a moment it held me, then I felt its cold iron slide through my fingers, felt myself falling backward. I heard a rushing sound in my ears and plunged into darkness.

seventeen

I opened my eyes in a white room with pale-striped drapes. It smelled like raspberry bathroom cleaner.

"Where am I?"

"With me."

I turned toward Matt's voice.

"How are you feeling?" he asked.

I lifted my head and glanced around. "Well, since I'm in a hospital, I can't be feeling too well."

He grinned. "You're talking like yourself, and you've been acting like yourself. The nurse said if you pulled out your IV one more time, she'd staple it to you."

"It's out," I observed.

"The doctor said that you'd come around soon enough, and then they'd irrigate you."

"Oh, that sounds like fun." I tried to sit up.

"Easy," he said, and slid his arm behind me to help.

I rested back against him. "Thanks. You don't want your arm back, do you?"

"Nah. Slide over." He sat next to me on the bed. It felt good, the way he kept me close.

"Do you remember anything?"

"Yeah." I took a deep breath. "If it was a dream, I'm crazy, and if it was real, some awful things have happened."

"Some awful things have happened," he said gently. "You may not want to talk about it yet."

"The sooner the better," I told him.

He leaned forward to study my face, then sat back again, convinced. "All right. You, Lydia, and I were at the mill, on the first floor. Do you remember our conversation?"

"You talked about who killed Avril, but it was confusing. The sounds and images kept overlapping. Sometimes I was in the past, sometimes the present."

"You were drugged."

"Drugged? But I didn't have anything to eat all day," I protested. "Just tea at Mrs. Riley's."

Matt said nothing, waiting for me to figure it out. I felt as if I'd just been punched in the stomach. "She did it. She did to me what she did to Avril."

He lay his cheek against my forehead. "I almost lost you a second time."

"I remember that she tried to keep you away from me. I thought she was protecting me."

"She didn't want me to interfere before the poison took full effect," he said.

I shivered. "She wanted to kill me, before I could kill her. I remember being at the top of the stairs. My foot slipped and I reached up for something. A pipe, but it gave way. I started falling. I don't remember landing, just falling."

One corner of Matt's mouth turned up in that smirky smile of his, then I noticed the wrap on his left ankle. "Oh, no! Tell me I didn't."

"Okay. You *didn't* come down like a ballerina," he said, then laughed at me. "It's just a sprain. But it's the last time I'm catching you, so don't try it again."

"Thank you," I said meekly. "How about Mrs. Riley—where is she? What has she told people?"

He didn't answer right away. I felt his arms tighten around me. "Megan, Lydia has died. The pipe struck her."

I went cold all over. "Oh, God!"

"It's all right," he said. "Everything's all right now."

"I did it," I whispered.

"It was an accident."

"But I did it!"

"You didn't mean to. You know that."

"Mrs. Riley said it would happen, intentional or not. Karma."

My eyes burned. Matt pulled my face against his and let my tears run down his cheeks.

Finally I reached for the tissue box.

"Okay?" he asked gently.

"For now."

"I'll be around later, too," he said.

I looked up into his eyes. "When did you know about us—about us back then?"

"I dreamed about you, saw your face, from the time I was nine or ten. When I got to high school, I talked to Lydia and she told me about reincarnation. I thought she was nuts. Then, when I described you, she said you looked like my great-aunt Avril. That's all I needed to hear—I was out of there.

"I dated every girl who'd go out with me, but I couldn't get interested in any of them. Finally—maybe it was sheer willpower—I stopped dreaming of you. A few months later Grandmother told me she had invited my cousin for a visit. I turned around and there you were." He framed my face with his hands.

"You looked stunned," I recalled.

"I was."

"I still find it strange that Grandmother asked me here."

"I know that she doesn't believe in reincarnation," Matt said. "Still, your resemblance to Avril unnerved her. Grandmother's a lot like you—she faces her fears—so she invited you. While we waited for you to come, she seemed so tormented, so obsessed with you, I disliked you before you arrived—at least I thought I did."

I laid my head on Matt's shoulder.

"Does Grandmother have any idea what's going on now?" I asked.

"She knows that Lydia killed Avril, that she shifted

her own motive for murdering Avril to Grandmother. Earlier today Sophie and Alex came to the house looking for you with information about redcreep. When I put together what they had learned with what Grandmother had told me the other night, I knew the timeline didn't work out. Grandmother gave the dose too early—and gave too little. Someone else had a hand in it. We told Grandmother that and she called Lydia. Jamie said his mother had gone to collect some plants at the mill. Which is where you told Sophie and Alex you would be. Sophie was scared, said she had feared all day that something would happen there. I rushed to the mill. Grandmother called 911."

He buried his face in my hair. "I know I've been tough on you, Megan. I did whatever I could to keep distance between us. It was useless. At the party how do you think I knew you were watching out for Sophie?"

"I must have been pretty obvious."

"And I was pretty busy watching you and Alex," he said. "I was so jealous of him I thought I'd explode."

I laughed, then covered my mouth.

He pulled away my hand and gazed at my mouth, as he had that night. "And then you tried to sell me on Sophie."

"I didn't know I had a chance." I touched the curve of his lips with the tip of my finger.

"Megan, I love you. I will always love you."

I swallowed hard.

"Scared?" he asked.

"Yeah. How about you?"

"Even more than the first time," he said. "I know what it feels like to lose you."

Then he bent his head and kissed me.

Sometime after Matt left, Grandmother came in. I had dozed off and wasn't aware of her until I felt her hand touch my hair, brushing it back from my face.

"You must get well," she said, her voice shaking. "Megan, you must heal."

I opened one eye. "Are you telling me what to do again?"

Grandmother stepped back quickly. I tried to catch her hand but couldn't.

"Sorry. I was just being funny, just making a joke—trying to." I struggled to sit up. "You sounded so serious, Grandmother."

"I was serious. You nearly died."

We both looked away.

"Thanks for calling emergency," I told her. "I owe you my life."

"You owe me nothing."

I frowned at her. "Because you don't want me to? Because that connects us somehow?"

A long uncomfortable silence followed.

I sighed. "It's going to take a while for us to get used to each other, isn't it?"

"I am who I am, Megan," she replied. "I'm old. I can't change now."

"Change?" I repeated. "I wasn't even going to try. Can't we just stay as we are and get used to each other?"

I saw the small flicker of light in her eyes and the corners of her mouth turn up a little. "That," she said, "may be feasible."

eighteen

despite what I said about staying the way we were, I changed. I, who have always believed in speaking my mind and made it my mission to uncover the truth, have found myself keeping secrets. Sometimes life is more complicated than the simple rules we make for it.

In the morning that followed my poisoning, Grandmother, Matt, and I agreed to keep silent. Jamie believed his mother had become mentally confused, unintentionally giving me something that made me ill. He came to the hospital to tell us that, even brought the teacup from which I had drunk, so it could be tested and the doctors would know how to treat me. But I had already been diagnosed with an overdose of redcreep. We threw the cup in the trash.

Sophie and Alex came to the hospital together that

day. I saw the brightness in Sophie's eyes, then the delicate chain around her neck.

"That pendant looks familiar," I said.

She smiled. "Alex bought it for me."

In the year since, they've become the best of friends again, and the best of sweethearts—again.

As for Grandmother, she, too, has changed, though I certainly wouldn't point it out to her. I suppose it's hard to keep your life the same when two extra grandsons, my rough-and-tumble brothers, come barreling through on holidays.

Matt's at Chase College now on a lacrosse scholarship. I'm applying to colleges in Maryland. And we're keeping another secret, though maybe not as well as we thought. Just the other day Jamie stopped me on High Street. "You know," he said. "I make wedding cakes."

about the author

A former high school and college teacher with a Ph.D. in English literature from the University of Rochester, ELIZABETH CHANDLER now writes full time and enjoys visiting schools to talk about the process of creating books. She has written numerous picture books for children under her real name, Mary Claire Helldorfer, as well as romances for teens under her pen name, Elizabeth Chandler. Her romance novels include *Hot Summer Nights, Love Happens, At First Sight, I Do,* and the romance-mystery trilogy *Kissed by an Angel,* published by Archway Paperbacks.

When not writing, Mary Claire enjoys biking, gardening, watching sports, and daydreaming. She has been a die-hard Oriole fan since she was a kid and a daydreamer for just as long. Mary Claire lives in Baltimore with her husband, Bob, and their cat, Puck.

DARK SECRETS™
by Elizabeth Chandler

Who is Megan? She's about to find out....
#1: Legacy of Lies

Megan thought she knew who she was.

Until she came to Grandmother's house.

Until she met Matt, who angered and attracted her as no boy ever had before.

Then she began having dreams again, of a life she never lived, a love she never

knew...a secret that threatened to drive her to the grave.

Home is where the horror is....
#2: Don't Tell

Lauren is coming home, eight years after her mother's mysterious drowning. They said

it was an accident. But the tabloids screamed murder. Aunt Jule was her only refuge,

the beloved second mother she's returning to see. But first Lauren stops at Wisteria's

annual street festival and meets Nick, a tease, a flirt, and a childhood playmate.

The day is almost perfect—until she realizes she's being watched.

A series of nasty "accidents" makes Lauren realize someone wants her dead.

And this time there's no place to run....

Archway Paperbacks
Published by Pocket Books

3027

Beware cheerleaders bearing gifts....

✷✶✷✶✷✶✷✶✷

NIGHT OF THE POMPON
by the teen sensation writer
Sarah Jett

Pompons aren't just for
pep rallies any more....

Who knows what evil lies beyond the oven door?
Jendra MacKenzie knows—it's a strangely powerful
pompon that turns bright-eyed cheerleaders into gray-
eyed monsters. But what she doesn't know is how to
explain the unusual events unfolding at the Davy
Crockett school ever since ultra-popular Tina
Shepard handed her a coyote head and made her the
cheerleading mascot. Who's responsible for the sudden disappearance of the last mascot, and the principal's pants...and the principal?

When Jendra searches for answers, she finds nothing
but trouble. Propelled by powers she can't control, she
winds up disco dancing on top of her desk, flying to a
faraway dentist's office, and dodging falling eighth-
graders in the second story girls' bathroom. If this
trend toward the bizarre continues, she might even
pass pre-algebra...unless the cheerleaders have something more sinister in mind....

✷ ✷ Archway Paperbacks
Published by Pocket Books
3045

Jeff Gottesfeld and Cherie Bennett's

MIRROR IMAGE

When does a dream become a nightmare?
Find out in MIRROR IMAGE as a teenage girl
finds a glittering meteorite, places it under her pillow,
and awakens to discover that her greatest wish
has come true…

STRANGER IN THE MIRROR

Is gorgeous as great as it looks?

RICH GIRL IN THE MIRROR

Watch out what you wish for…

STAR IN THE MIRROR

Sometimes it's fun to play the part

of someone you're not

…until real life takes center stage.

FLIRT IN THE MIRROR

… From tongue-tied girl to the ultimate flirt queen.

From Archway Paperbacks

Published by Pocket Books

2312

Todd Strasser's

HERE COMES HEAVENLY

Here Comes Heavenly

She just appeared out of nowhere. Spiky purple hair, tons of
earrings and rings. Hoops through her eyebrow and nostril,
and tattoos on both arms. She said her name was Heavenly
Litebody. Our nanny. Nanny???

Dance Magic

Heavenly is cool and punk. She sure isn't the nanny our
parents wanted for my baby brother, Tyler. And what's with
all those ladybugs?

Pastabilities

Heavenly Litebody goes to Italy with the family and causes all
kinds of merriment! But...is the land of *amore* ready for her?

Spell Danger

Kit has to find a way to keep Heavenly Litebody, the
Rands' magical, mysterious nanny from leaving the
family forever.

Available from Archway Paperbacks
Published by Pocket Books

2307.01